EXTREM ...ES

6

Man-Eater

JUSTIN D'ATH

Kane Miller
A DIVISION OF EDC PUBLISHING

Extreme Adventures

Book 1 – Crocodile Attack
Book 2 – Bushfire Rescue
Book 3 – Shark Bait
Book 4 – Scorpion Sting
Book 5 – Spider Bite
Book 6 – Man-Eater

First American Edition 2011
Kane Miller, A Division of EDC Publishing

First published in 2007 by Penguin Group (Australia)
Text copyright © Justin D'Ath, 2007

Library of Congress Control Number: 2010934688

Printed and bound in the United States of America
1 2 3 4 5 6 7 8 9 10
ISBN: 978-1-61067-011-1

For my brother Bill, who introduced me to the world of **The Jungle Book**

(1)

DEEP TROUBLE

There was a low, trembly rumble, like the sound of distant thunder.

Or like a diesel engine starting up.

Oh, no! The bus was going without me!

I quickly adjusted my clothing and stepped out from behind the fig tree where I'd gone for privacy. And stopped in my tracks.

Shishkebab!

The baby elephant looked startled, too. I guess it had never come face to face with a human before. Only ten feet separated us. It flapped its oversized ears and lifted its stubby, pink-tipped trunk in my direction.

Please don't trumpet, I prayed.

Because the calf wasn't alone. Another elephant stood in the thorn bushes behind it. The calf's mother. She was massive. As big as a dump truck. With tusks longer than my arms. It was a miracle she hadn't seen me – I was standing in plain view. She was busily picking up fallen figs with her long, nimble trunk and lifting them one by one to her mouth.

Instead of sounding the alarm, the calf tested the air for my scent. I backed away slowly, keeping a wary eye on the mother, then slid around the tree and flattened myself against its lumpy gray bark. But the calf followed me. It began sniffing me all over, like a curious puppy.

But here's the difference: Puppies don't weigh three hundred pounds, and their mothers aren't liable to pulverize any living thing that comes within sixty feet of their calves. I was *zero* feet from this calf!

"Buzz off!" I whispered, pushing its fat, little trunk away.

Then I heard the rumbling noise again, and a huge gray shape – like a moving wall – passed slowly across a gap in a hedge of thorn bushes. More rumbling came from my right. Now I knew what was causing it – elephants. Everywhere I looked, I saw patches of wrinkly gray skin through the head-high undergrowth. It didn't seem real. Thirty-six hours ago I'd been sitting at our kitchen table back home in Australia, writing a speech about saving bilbies. Now here I was in a remote corner of eastern Africa, surrounded by wild elephants!

And one was head-butting me. The calf was only being curious, but it was as big as a Shetland pony and nearly breaking my ribs. I placed both hands on its broad, leathery forehead and pushed with all my might. The calf seemed to think it was a game. It leaned against my hands and pushed the other way.

That was when the *real* diesel engine started up. I'd come to Tanzania to represent Australia at the first ever International Youth for Wildlife Conference. The bus that was taking me to Marusha (where I had to give my speech the following day) had made a five-minute bathroom stop in the middle of a game reserve. Now the bus was ready to leave, and I couldn't go back to it. The baby elephant had me trapped. I wanted to call for help, but that would have alerted the other elephants to my presence. If the calf's mother found me having a pushing contest with her baby, I was history.

The bus driver sounded the horn. It was one of those trick horns that played a tune – five shrill notes that repeated three times. A noise that had no place in the African bush. It startled the elephants. Sticks snapped, leaves rustled, the ground trembled. All around me, huge gray forms went swaying off through the trees.

The calf seemed confused. It backed away from me and turned around, raising its trunk above its head in a fat gray question mark.

"Go after them," I said, giving it a slap on the rump. "Your mum –"

I was about to say, *your mum went that-a-way*, when an ear-splitting shriek silenced me. It was louder than the bus's musical horn. But unlike the horn, this noise *did* belong in the African bush.

It was the sound of an elephant trumpeting.

My insides turned to jelly. I'd been wrong about the mother elephant: She hadn't run off with the others. She was only fifteen feet away. Looking directly at me. And she didn't look happy. Not only had she caught me with her baby, but she'd seen me smack it on the backside.

I was in deep trouble.

2

WHOMP! THUMP! CRUNCH! WHAM! THWACK!

The mother elephant tossed her huge head, flapped her ears like two car doors, and shot a blast of air through her trunk that blew down a shower of figs from the tree above us.

Then she charged.

She was unbelievably fast. I only got halfway around the fig tree before – *whomp!* – a mighty blow from her trunk knocked me off my feet.

I hit the ground rolling. It was lucky I did because an enormous white tusk rammed into the earth exactly where I'd landed. A second one buried itself next to my hip. The elephant loomed above me, blocking out the sky. I raised both hands to protect myself, but it was like trying to hold up a falling building.

Thump!

Everything went dark. The elephant's huge, bristly head pressed against my face and chest and stomach, grinding violently from side to side. She was trying to crush me, but it wasn't working. Two massive roots sloped down from the tree trunk, one on either side of me, preventing my four-ton assailant from pressing all the way down. But she had me pinned. The only thing I could move was my right leg. I kicked upwards. My foot hit something soft. The elephant let out a shriek of rage and wrenched her tusks free, tearing up two huge clods of earth. Dust filled the air with a dense red fog. For a moment I couldn't see anything. Nor could the elephant. She slammed her head back down – *crunch!* – but I was no longer there.

I was commando crawling along the ground underneath the gray ceiling of her belly, my eyes fixed on the hazy wedge of daylight between her back legs.

She was smart. Before I could crawl out from under her, she shuffled backwards and sideways, trying to trample me. Her feet were like pile drivers.

The ground shook. It was an elephant earthquake, nine on the Richter scale. I twisted and rolled to avoid her huge, stomping feet. Dust billowed. It was hard to see. A foot the size of a tree stump came swinging towards me. It grazed my back, pinning the tail of my *Youth for Wildlife* shirt to the ground. Fabric ripped. I wrenched myself free and bumped into another foot. Luckily, this one was going up, not down. I wriggled the other way. Another foot came slamming down. I flung myself sideways.

A few yards to my right was a dense tangle of thorn bushes. It looked prickly and nearly impenetrable, but it was my only chance of escape. I scrambled upright and made a break for it, but the elephant was too quick. She pivoted her rear end like a jackknifing semi-trailer, knocking me off balance. I grabbed her tail to stop myself falling, then hung on for my life as she whirled around after me. My feet left the ground, and I spun in a huge circle. The elephant couldn't quite reach me with her extended trunk. She turned faster and faster, trying to catch up. It must have looked comical – the elephant spinning around with me swinging from her tail – but there was nothing funny about it. If I let go, I was dead.

Wham!

Everything stopped. I found myself surrounded by leaves and prickles and vines.

Where was I?

Something moved underneath me. I swiveled my head around.

Holy guacamole! I was lying spread-eagle on top of the baby elephant.

It struggled to its feet in a tangle of undergrowth, lifting me up, too. I realized what had happened: I'd lost my grip on the mother's tail and slammed into her calf. The collision had sent us both crashing into the thorn bushes.

So where's the mother? asked a little voice in my head.

A massive shadow fell over me.

Thwack!

3

THE MEANEST ANIMAL
IN THE WORLD

Eight inches to the left, and the tusk would have passed clean through my chest and out the other side. But the mother elephant was dizzy from chasing her tail, and her aim was off. Instead of turning me into a human kebab, the side of her left tusk struck me a glancing blow to the shoulder, toppling me off the calf's back. I landed next to its feet and crouched there, not moving. The calf was trapped between me and its mother, and all around us was a wall of undergrowth, higher than the calf's back and woven together with prickly vines. As long as I stayed where I was, the mother couldn't get me.

Wrong. I'd forgotten about her trunk. *Whuff,*

whuff, snuffle. A big, wet suction pump went sliding across my back, searching for something to grab onto. Desperately, I wriggled right under the calf, squeezing into the small gap between its four stubby legs and soft, round belly. Now the mother couldn't get her trunk around me. But her calf could. Reaching between its front legs, it tried grabbing me by the neck. I pressed my chin against my chest to protect my throat. But the calf slid its trunk inside my shirt collar. Bunching the fabric together in a big, tight knot, it started pulling. It was only a baby, but it was a *big* baby. And strong. The shirt tightened around my neck like a hangman's noose. I couldn't breathe.

Frantically, I began ripping the buttons undone. It was either take my shirt off or be strangled. But this opened me up to another line of attack. As I dragged one of my arms out of its shirt sleeve, the mother elephant got me by the elbow. And started pulling.

That was when I heard the strange, rattling noise.

I didn't pay much attention at first because I had a two-way struggle on my hands – one to free myself from the shirt before the calf strangled me, the other to free my elbow from the mother's trunk before she dislocated my arm.

The rattling noise changed pitch and grew louder. And the air filled with a truly disgusting stink.

The calf let go of my shirt and gave a frightened squeal. This was too much for the mother elephant; she released my arm and began running her trunk all over her baby, trying to find out what was wrong. I raised my head.

Three feet away, framed in the arch of the calf's front legs, crouched the weirdest-looking animal I'd ever seen. At first I thought it was a skunk. That would account for the stink. The color was right, too – black and white – but this animal seemed bigger than the skunks I'd seen on TV. It looked like a cross between a ferret and a Tasmanian devil, only it was bigger than a ferret and uglier than a devil. It had no ears, just holes in the sides of its head like a lizard. And it looked *mean*. When it saw me watching, the mystery creature wrinkled its scarred black nose and bared its teeth. They were long and pointed like a crocodile's. Then it made the rattling noise I'd heard earlier – its way of growling, I guess – and darted towards me.

It was a honey badger, I've found out since. They are the meanest animals in the world. Even though they're no bigger than corgis, honey badgers have been known to chase lions from their kills. They even attack animals as large as Cape buffalos, creeping up when they're asleep and biting an artery so they bleed to death. They're not afraid of anything. Not even elephants.

They should be. Elephants aren't afraid of anything either – especially not mother elephants whose calves are in danger – and they have a size advantage. The honey badger had made a mistake. It had threatened the baby elephant (and me) when the mother was standing right next to us. Maybe it hadn't realized the mother was there. It soon found out.

When the honey badger began its rush forward, the mother elephant saw the movement. Her trunk came flying down like a giant lasso. It curled around the honey badger and flung it high into the air. For a moment there was silence, then something thumped back to earth about fifty feet away. Above me, the mother elephant trumpeted in victory.

Still crouched under her baby, I dragged my shirt all the way off. There wasn't a moment to lose. I was next on the mother's hit list. The honey badger had bought me some time, but no more than a few seconds.

I had just tied the shirt's sleeves together when the big elephant's trunk came looking for me again. This time I made no attempt to get out of the way. I looped the loosely knotted shirt around the tip of her trunk and pulled the sleeves as tight as I could. The noose snapped closed. Gotcha!

The elephant bellowed in surprise. Or tried to. But my shirt was knotted around her trunk like a tourniquet, constricting her nostrils and blocking the flow of air. All that came out was a wheezing, raspberry sound.

She went totally psycho. Her trunk, with my *Youth for Wildlife* shirt attached, disappeared from view. Bushes crunched, dust flew, the ground shook. It was like a tornado, an earthquake and an avalanche all at once, as the enraged elephant went crashing off into the distance, wheezing and honking and blowing giant raspberries. Free to move at last, her calf reversed away from me, spun around and went trotting out of the thorn bushes after its mother.

I went in the other direction. Rather than leave the safety of the thorn bushes, I burrowed my way further in. It was easier than I expected. Where the honey badger had first appeared, there was a small, arched opening between the stems of two bushes. I later found out it was the mouth of a secret tunnel through the undergrowth, used by small animals like honey badgers, hyraxes and mongooses. That's probably why the honey badger had threatened the baby elephant and me. We were blocking its path, and honey badgers don't back down.

The tunnel was a tight fit and very prickly against my bare back. But prickles were the least of my worries as I dragged myself along on my belly and elbows, moving deeper and deeper into the thicket. My idea was to stop somewhere near the middle and hope the mother elephant didn't come looking for me once she got the shirt off her trunk. It was a good idea, but I didn't get to put it into practice. Because there was another creature in the thorn thicket that afternoon. Something much more scary than a honey badger.

And it was coming along the tunnel in the other direction.

STAY OUT OF MY WAY, DUDE!

I don't know what it is about me and snakes. Wherever I go – the flood plains of the Northern Territory, the New South Wales high country, the Great Barrier Reef – I seem to run into them. So when I came face to face with one in the middle of the thorn bushes in Tanzania, Africa, I shouldn't have been surprised. But I nearly jumped out of my skin. Because I'd never seen a live cobra before, and they're scary. Especially up close. This one was less than six feet away. Its head was raised, its hood was spread, and its little black eyes seemed to bore right into mine.

It was blocking the tunnel. There was nowhere to go except forwards or backwards. I could hear the elephant behind me. She was trumpeting now (she must have gotten my shirt off her trunk), and it sounded like she was coming in my direction. There was nothing I could do except keep burrowing forward.

My brother Nathan reckons snakes won't attack a human unless they're cornered or feel threatened. He should know, he's a tour guide for an outdoor adventure company. But that's in Australia. This was Africa.

The cobra wasn't cornered. It was a snake – it didn't need to travel along the tunnel. But I did, and the thicket hemmed me in like a long, prickly cage. Taking a deep breath to calm myself, I wriggled forwards a few more inches. Towards the snake. It held its ground. Its head rocked slowly back and forth atop its tall, scaly neck. It flickered its black, Y-shaped tongue at me.

I stopped about five feet short of the cobra. Too far away for it to strike.

"C'mon, give me a break," I whispered. "I just want to get past you."

The elephant trumpeted again. She sounded really close. Bushes crunched; the ground shook.

Snakes are deaf – the cobra didn't hear anything. But it felt the vibrations of the approaching elephant. To a snake, vibrations mean danger. And danger means threat. The cobra's small reptilian brain put two and two together and came up with the totally wrong conclusion: that *I* was the threat.

I had no idea what was going on in the snake's head. I was more worried about the elephant behind me than the cobra in front. So when the snake opened its mouth and seemed to yawn, I was totally unprepared for what happened next.

A soft spray, like gentle raindrops, touched my face. The next moment … *agony!* My left eye was *burning!* It felt like I'd been sprayed with acid.

The snake, I realized too late, was a spitting cobra. They spit venom as a defense mechanism, aiming at the eyes, and they seldom miss. While their victim writhes in agony, the cobra makes its getaway. Which was the only good thing about what happened. After it sprayed me, the snake darted off into the thicket. I didn't even see it go – I was in too much pain. My eye was *on fire!*

There was an ear-splitting, trumpeting sound just behind me. For a moment I forgot about my eye.

I don't recall much about getting out of the thorn thicket, only that I managed it in double-quick time. I remember seeing a small circle of daylight ahead, then scrambling to my feet and dashing across an open space to a large, umbrella-shaped acacia tree. Ducking behind it, I pressed my back against the scratchy bark and hoped the elephant hadn't seen me. I could hear her not far away, crashing around in the thorn bushes like a bulldozer doing burnouts. I wondered how good her sense of smell was. Could she track my scent to the tree?

I listened and waited, my heart going flat out. There was another tree about twenty-five feet away, and just past it was a clump of plants like giant aloe veras. They would be good to hide behind. But could I reach them without the elephant seeing me? It wasn't a risk I wanted to take.

My eye was killing me. I had to wash the venom out. There were two water bottles in my backpack, but I'd left it on the bus. I turned my head, anxiously scanning the surrounding landscape with my unaffected eye. Where was the road? I'd lost all sense of direction. *Toot the horn again*, I thought, trying to send a telepathic message to the bus driver.

Get real! said a more logical part of my mind. *How long is it since you've even heard the bus?*

But the driver wouldn't leave without me! I argued with myself.

He might, said my mind, *if he didn't realize you weren't on it.*

The bus had been seriously overcrowded – there were about fifty passengers, twice as many as the number of seats. I'd been traveling alone, squashed in next to a crate of chickens right down at the back. And I wasn't the only white passenger – there were some backpackers from Germany and a young Italian couple – so nobody might have noticed that I didn't get back on.

A sudden movement near my feet made me forget about the bus. I flattened myself against the tree trunk as a familiar black-and-white animal came shuffling past. The honey badger was limping slightly, and its fur was matted with dirt, but it looked as mean as ever. When it saw me it gave a low, rattling growl, as if to say, *stay out of my way, dude, if you know what's good for you!* Then it limped off towards the giant aloe vera plants, dragging the mangled body of a dead cobra behind it.

⑤

DANGEROUS COUNTRY

It was two or three minutes since the mother elephant had last trumpeted. I could no longer hear her stomping around among the thorn bushes. Where was she?

I peered around the tree trunk, hoping she had gone. No such luck. The massive animal stood only thirty feet away, towering over the remains of the thicket, which looked like a demolition site. No wonder the honey badger had gone somewhere else to eat its dinner. As I spied on her from my hiding place, the elephant raised her trunk and sniffed the air. A scrap of frayed blue fabric dangled from one of her tusks. I gave a little shiver. That would have been me if I'd stayed in the thorn bushes.

Slowly, I edged back out of sight and leaned against the tree trunk, rubbing my sore eye. The pain was getting worse. I had to find water. But I was trapped behind the tree until the elephant went away. *If* she went away. I could hear a *whoosh whoosh* sound as she tested the air for my scent.

Then I heard something else – a rumbling noise, like distant thunder. The elephant heard it, too. She trumpeted softly, calling to her calf. There was an answering squeal from the trees over to my right, but I was more interested in the rumbling sound. It grew louder with every passing moment. And the louder it became, the less it sounded like thunder. Or like rumbling elephants.

It was the thrum of tires on a dirt road.

Before I realized what I was doing, I'd left my hiding place behind the acacia and was running flat out towards the sound. Even if the mother elephant chased me, I reckoned I could beat her to the road. The approaching vehicle sounded close. A cloud of dust rose between the trees ahead. Sunlight flashed on a windshield. The next moment, I was charging out onto the dirt road, waving my arms above my head and screaming like a madman, *"Stop, stop, stop!"*

It was a battered gray Land Rover with a brown canvas canopy on the back. It nearly mowed me down, skidding to a standstill with less than three feet to spare. Dust swirled everywhere.

"Are you crazy? I nearly hit you!" a man's voice yelled.

I ran around the other side of the Land Rover, putting it between me and the forest.

"Help! Let me in!" I cried. "An elephant's chasing me!"

The door flew open, and a short, thick-set white man jumped out. He pumped a bullet into the breech of a big hunting rifle. It was a .460 Weatherby Magnum – this man meant business.

"Where is it?" he asked.

"Just down there," I said, pointing back the way I'd come.

The dust slowly cleared, but there was no sign of the elephant. The man lowered his rifle.

"Are you sure you weren't imagining things?"

"She must have stayed with her calf," I said. My heart fluttered with relief. "Could I have some water, please? A cobra sprayed me in the eye. It really hurts!"

The man studied me for a few moments, his own eyes narrowed, and for the first time I realized how terrible I must have looked: no shirt, scratches and dirt all over me, my left eye swollen nearly all the way shut. He turned and spoke in Swahili to two native Africans waiting in the Land Rover's dusty cab. One of them tossed me a water bottle. As I rinsed my eye, the three men had a long conversation in Swahili. I knew they were talking about me because I heard *mzungu*, the word for "white man," repeated several times. I recognized another word, too – *tembo*, which means "elephant."

"What are you doing here?" asked the other *mzungu*, when I'd finished sluicing my eye with water. It felt much better.

I explained what had happened, then asked, "Are you going as far as Marusha?"

"Sorry, chum," said the white man, sliding back the rifle's bolt and removing the big, soft-nosed bullet. "We're headed the other way."

He was lying – the Land Rover had been traveling in the same direction as the bus. But something in the man's expression reminded me of the honey badger, and I knew better than to argue.

"Could you take me to the next village?" I asked.

One of the men in the Land Rover interrupted. "*Tembo!*" he hissed, pointing through the dusty windshield.

I spun around, ready to run, but the elephant was two hundred yards away, crossing the road towards a grove of fever trees on the other side. The calf trotted behind her, the tip of its fat, little trunk wrapped around its mother's tail.

"See that piece of blue rag on her tusk?" I said. "That used to be my shirt."

I don't think anyone heard me. Certainly not the white man – he was too busy reloading his rifle. I felt my mouth drop open as he raised it and took aim at the mother elephant.

"Hey, don't shoot her!" I cried, knocking the rifle to one side.

Boom!

The .460 Weatherby Magnum is the most powerful hunting rifle in the world. The recoil nearly knocked the man over backwards. A white spray of wood and bark chips exploded from the trunk of a tree a hundred and fifty feet away, and a huge branch fell across the road. The man shouted and pumped another bullet into his weapon, but by the time he raised it again the elephants had disappeared into the forest. He turned on me, his face bright red.

"What did you think you were doing?" he roared, spraying me with spit.

I took a step backwards. "Isn't this a game reserve?" I stammered. "I thought elephants were protected."

The man's face was nearly purple with rage. He half-raised his rifle. For a scary moment I thought he was going to shoot me. Instead, he shouted, "*I was protecting you, you moron!*"

"But she wasn't chasing me anymore," I said, looking at the man, not at the big, ugly rifle. "I didn't want you to shoot her. She had a baby."

He took a deep breath and seemed to calm himself. Clicking the rifle's safety catch, he addressed me in a low, steely voice. "A word of advice, Aussie. Go back home. This is dangerous country. A boy like you could wind up dead."

It wasn't advice, it was a warning. The man and I stared at each other for a few more seconds, neither of us speaking. I think he wanted me to back down and say I was sorry for interfering, but no way in the world was I going to do that. Especially not to a man with a .460 Weatherby Magnum. I had come to Africa because of my concern for animals, and men like him were part of the problem.

Finally, he climbed back into the Land Rover, and it roared off down the road. It swerved around the fallen branch, then slowed and went bumping off into the trees exactly where the two elephants had disappeared.

Only then did it dawn on me why the man had been so angry. And why he'd threatened me. He and his two companions were poachers. Ivory hunters.

Go, elephants! I urged them in my mind. *It's not safe around here.*

It wasn't safe for me, either. The ivory hunter was right – this was dangerous country. Already I'd been nearly flattened by an elephant, half-blinded by a spitting cobra, and threatened by a man with an elephant gun.

What next? I wondered, looking nervously into the dusty yellow forest that flanked the road.

A pair of evil-looking brown eyes stared back.

6

JAWS OF DESTRUCTION

Most animals will run away at the sound of a gunshot. Not hyenas. When they hear a rifle, more often than not they'll come to see what the hunter has killed. And to clean up whatever he leaves behind. Hyenas have the most powerful jaws of any creature in the animal kingdom. They can crunch through even the largest bones as if they were twigs. They will eat every part of a dead animal, including its horns, hooves and teeth. They are the ultimate scavengers.

They are also highly proficient hunters. They kill about ninety-five percent of the animals they eat. Most people don't know that. I didn't know that at the time. I didn't think I was in any danger as the big, spotted hyena emerged from the bushes and came slinking towards me. It stopped in the tall yellow grass about fifty feet away.

"There's nothing for you here," I said. "Nobody shot anything."

The hyena held its ground. It looked like a cross between a very large dog and a leopard. I began to feel uneasy.

"Scram!" I said loudly. I picked up a small stone and threw it.

I didn't aim directly at the hyena; I only wanted to scare it. The hyena turned to see where the stone landed, then looked at me again. It seemed to be frowning.

"Scram," I repeated, more softly this time, and rubbed my eye. The effects of the water were beginning to wear off, and it was starting to sting again. It was so swollen, I could barely see out of it.

The hyena watched me closely. It seemed interested when I rubbed my eye. Did it sense that I was injured? Quickly, I lowered my hand and returned its bold stare, trying my best not to squint. I knew hyenas preyed on creatures that were hurt and weak.

I might have been hurt, but I wasn't weak. I

picked up another stone. This time I didn't aim to miss. The hyena let out a strange, bawling sound – almost like a human baby crying – and went loping off into the trees. I felt bad for hitting it, but my own safety came first. I couldn't take any chances. This was Africa.

Now that the hyena was gone, I could safely rub my eye again. The pain was getting worse. It felt like someone had wrapped my eyeball in barbed wire and pulled the ends tight. And my right eye felt slightly itchy, too, which was seriously scary. If it swelled shut like the other one, I'd be totally helpless. Hyena food. I had to find my way to a hospital.

The bus had passed through a small village about half an hour before we stopped. I could walk back there. They might have a doctor. At the very least, there would be water to give my eye another wash. Both eyes. My right eye was definitely beginning to itch. Some of the cobra's venom must have gotten into it as well.

Keeping to the middle of the road, I set off back the way we'd come. Half an hour by bus would take roughly two hours on foot. But I didn't think I would have to walk all the way. Sooner or later another vehicle would come along. Someone would give me a lift.

But would they arrive in time? After fifteen minutes my bad eye was hurting so much I could hardly stand it. It was swollen completely shut, and tears streamed down my face in a steady flow. I staggered along in a daze, half-delirious with pain. Every footstep produced an excruciating, red-hot explosion at the back of my left eye, accompanied by a smaller, duller pain behind my right. My vision was down to one eye, and that was becoming blurry, too. When a troop of baboons went scampering across the road two hundred feet ahead, I thought they were children.

"Hey!" I yelled. "Where's your village? I need a doctor!"

Only when one of the "children" shot up a skinny tree and went swinging out along a branch did I realize my mistake. *Good one, Sam. Talking to monkeys.*

There was a cackle of maniacal laughter behind me, as if someone was sharing the joke. My skin prickled, and I turned around. The hyenas were about two hundred yards away, trotting boldly down the middle of the road. They stopped when they saw me watching. My vision was fuzzy, but I counted six of them, including a half-grown cub. Were they following me, or were they simply going in the same direction? I picked up a stone and hurled it towards them. The stone landed far short of the hyenas, but it had the desired effect – all six animals went slinking off into the roadside scrub.

I resumed walking, faster than before. Both eyes were throbbing, but I forced myself not to rub them. I held my head high and resisted the urge to look over my shoulder. If the hyenas were watching, I didn't want them to see that I was scared. Or that I was injured. My whole head throbbed. It was hard to think about anything other than the pain.

So when I saw the river, my only thought was, *water to rinse my eyes!* I forgot that the bus had driven past this very same river about one hour earlier.

And I forgot what I'd seen *in* the river.

7

BOULDERS

The river was three hundred yards from the road. It wound its way along the edge of a wide, grassy plain bordered by a semicircle of distant hills. Herds of wildebeest, zebra and antelope grazed on the open grassland, but I didn't pay much attention to them as I staggered half-blind down the long, scrub-dotted slope towards the river. The water was toffee brown and partially hidden behind a screen of tall papyrus reeds. I crashed through the reeds, went skating out of control down the steep, slippery bank, and landed waist-deep in the river. Plunging my face under, I peeled back the swollen lids of my left eye with my thumb and forefinger and allowed the cool brown water to wash over the inflamed cornea. Boy, it felt good! I stayed underwater for as long as I could hold my breath, then came up whooping and gasping for air.

Holy guacamole!

Now I remembered what I'd seen in the river when the bus drove past – hippos. I was face to face with one. The huge, snoozing animal was immersed up to its nostrils and eyelashes in the water. It was almost close enough to touch. Slowly, I backed away, all too aware that hippos kill more humans than any other animal in Africa. And nearly bumped into a big brown-and-pink boulder. A boulder with ears, eyes and nostrils. A boulder with a mouth like the entrance to the Sydney Harbor Tunnel. That's how big it looked when the second hippo rose out of the water like a breaching whale and took a snap at me.

Clunk!

Missed by an inch. I threw myself sideways, lost my footing on the slimy river bottom and went under. When I came up again, spitting water and blinking mud and silt from my single working eye, three hippos were coming at me, all from different directions. I scrambled backwards up the bank, slithering and sliding, and fell bottom-first into the wet, gooey mud at the top. Much to my relief, none of my pursuers followed me out of the water. One came churning towards the bank like a hydrofoil, but stopped six feet from shore. It stood watching me get up and stagger off into the reeds. The other two sank back into the river and became boulders again.

Phew!

My relief only lasted five seconds. That's how long it took to fight my way back through the reeds. When I came out the other side, dripping, coughing and shivering from my narrow escape, I skidded to a standstill.

There was another hippo on land.

This one must have been asleep under a tree when I'd come down the hill. I must have stumbled right past it in my half-blind rush to get to the river. Now I could see again, and the hippo was wide awake. Even worse, it was rushing towards me at about thirty miles per hour! Behind it were six hyenas, spread out in a line, also running. They no longer looked like scavengers; they looked like predators, one hundred percent. It wasn't clear what they were chasing – the hippo or me – but I didn't wait to find out. I turned and ran. Back through the reeds. Back to the river.

This time I wasn't half out of my mind with pain. And this time I could see clearly enough with my right eye. The river was about sixty-five feet wide and dotted with hippos from one steep, muddy bank to the other. Only their ears, nostrils and backs were visible above the water, giving them the appearance of boulders.

I took one last look over my shoulder, glimpsed the other hippo and the six hyenas smashing through the reeds behind me, and leapt onto the nearest "boulder."

⑧

TOTALLY OVER THE TOP

I'd been worried they might be slippery, but the hippos' skin felt like rubber. My sneakers got a good grip. I jumped from one snoozing animal to the next, skipping from back to back nearly all the way to the other side of the river. Surprise worked in my favor. Most of the hippos were sleeping – they didn't know I was coming until my sneakers touched down on their backs, and by then it was too late. They awoke with a jerk and snapped at me with their huge jaws, but I was already gone, flying through the air towards the unsuspecting hippo snoozing next to them.

I should never have tried it. Using live hippos as stepping stones – *crazy!* Three-quarters of the way across, things went wrong. A hippo opened its eyes and saw me just as I launched myself off the back of its neighbor. It swung its barrel-like head around to meet me. I couldn't stop myself. Already I was halfway across the gap in midair, my legs helplessly back-pedaling. The hippo opened its cavernous mouth, and my leading foot went straight in.

I thought I was dead. I would have been, too, had the hippo closed its mouth fast enough. My momentum saved me. I'd been skipping across the hippos like a triple jumper, gaining speed with every step. By the time I reached the last one, I was going flat out. A nanosecond after my foot went into the hippo's mouth, the rest of me slammed, knees-first, into its raised upper jaw. The collision forced its jaw back and spun me over its head in a forward flip. For a moment I was upside down, looking directly into the hippo's surprised brown eyes, then I completed my somersault and landed with a huge splash in the river behind it.

Now there was nothing between me and the bank except ten feet of water. That might not sound far, but even without looking over my shoulder I knew there were at least six angry hippos closing in. And if it came to a swimming race between me and the hippos, there was no chance that I could win. So I dived.

Instead of heading straight for the shore, I turned downriver, kicking my way through the murky brown water as fast as I could. I nearly didn't make it. With a surge of bubbles, a huge, dark shape swept past me like a submarine. I went limp for a moment, pretending to be a piece of driftwood, then continued downriver as soon as the coast was clear. At least I hoped it was downriver – I couldn't see anything.

It was hard swimming in my sneakers, and I was running out of breath. But if I came up for air, the hippos would see me. So I veered to the right, hoping to reach the bank before I had to breathe. Suddenly, I found myself tangled in slimy ropes. I was caught in a fishing net!

Don't panic, I cautioned myself. If I panicked, I would become even more tangled in the ropes, and I'd drown for sure. My first priority was air. I had to get to the surface and breathe. Then I would worry about freeing myself from the net and crawling out of the river – hopefully before the hippos caught up with me. The odds weren't good, but there wasn't time to think about it. I only had about three more seconds before my lungs caved in.

Placing both feet in the soft mud of the river bottom, I pushed myself up through the net. It was easier than I expected. The slippery ropes slid out of the way without any resistance, and my head broke through into daylight and sweet, glorious, life-giving air. I greedily filled my lungs, then sank back down to nose-level to take stock of my situation. I was surrounded by reeds, crouching in about five feet of water. It was the reeds that had tangled around me, rather than a net. In reality, they had saved my life. They screened me from the rest of the river, where the angry hippos still splashed and grunted as they continued their search for me. One was only a few yards away. I saw the tops of the reeds jiggling wildly from side to side, then a wash of tall brown ripples came sloshing through the stems towards me. I had to get out of the river. Fast!

But how? Even though I was quite close to shore, the bank looked higher and steeper than it had upstream. Luckily, the reeds provided me with cover as I edged away from the nearest hippo. A little further downstream, I found the perfect place to get out – a narrow, muddy pathway carved into the bank like a miniature boat ramp. As I pushed my way through the reeds towards it, half-crawling, half-swimming, one of my hands struck something hard in the cool, oozy mud of the river bottom. Something that moved.

Crunch!

Stifling a yelp of pain, I dragged my hand out of the water. Hooley dooly! A large green freshwater crayfish dangled by one over-sized claw from my right thumb. I whacked it with my other hand, sending the crayfish spinning away. But the claw stayed behind, still latched onto my thumb like a set of spring-loaded pliers. I flicked it off, then crawled out of the river. The crayfish had landed on the shore, near the bottom of the miniature boat ramp, and lay on its back, snapping at me with its remaining claw. I edged carefully past it, then scrambled up the narrow pathway that was cut so conveniently into the steep bank of the river. I was nearly at the top when a series of pictures flashed into my mind – memories of similar muddy ramps I'd seen on river banks in the Top End of Australia. I remembered my big bother taking me to see one when I was seven or eight years old.

"Guess what made that, Sam."

"I don't know."

"A crocodile," Nathan said. "It's where they slide down into the water."

Usually it makes me smile when I remember Nathan teaching me about the bush when I was little. But not this time. I couldn't have felt less like smiling.

Slowly, I raised my head and looked up the wet, muddy ramp above me.

Crikey! At the top, returning my stare, was a crocodile.

And unlike me, it definitely seemed to be smiling.

9

EATING MACHINE

I didn't know anything about African crocodiles. In Australia, the freshwater ones aren't dangerous. But this looked more like an Australian saltwater crocodile, and they *are*. It was much smaller than a salty, though – no more than six and a half feet long, and nearly half of that was tail. Perhaps it was only young. But whether it was fully grown or not made no difference – I was on the crocodile's slide, directly between it and the river. *Not* a good place to be.

Slowly, I backed down towards the water. The crocodile watched me. It didn't move. A couple of flies buzzed around its snout. There was a small gray-and-white feather stuck to one of the pointy teeth in the gap between its jaws – it must have recently eaten a bird. I hoped it was a big bird, and the crocodile was full.

Stay where you are, crocodile, said a little voice in my head, as I slithered slowly back down the slide. *I'm way too big for you to eat.*

Then I put my hand on something hard. Something that moved.

Crunch!

Oooooow! The crayfish was attached to my thumb again – my left thumb, this time. I tried shaking it off, but the pesky thing hung on. I went to grab it with my other hand. As I did, the crocodile woke from its trance. With a guttural hiss, it opened its long, toothy mouth and launched itself down its slipway.

If I'd had my wits about me, I would have rolled sideways – off the crocodile's slide and out of its way. But there wasn't time to think. Anyway, I was down to one eye and suffering from a bad case of tunnel vision – and when you're in a tunnel you can only go forwards or backwards. I was already going backwards, but not fast enough. The crocodile was going to catch me in about two seconds. In desperation, I threw the crayfish.

Crocodiles are like dinosaurs – compared to their body size, their brains are miniscule. They act on instinct, not brain power. And because they're at the top of the food chain, most of their instincts revolve around eating. They are eating machines. When the crayfish flew into its mouth, twenty million years of evolution kicked in, and the crocodile snapped its jaws shut.

Chomp!

Half a second. That was the margin between me losing a hand or an arm, or the crayfish losing its life. It died for a good cause. But I wasn't out of danger yet.

The crocodile's mouth might have been closed, but the reptile kept coming. It slammed into me like a torpedo. Somehow I got on top of it and applied a headlock before it could twist around and bite me, but its momentum carried us both into the river.

We went under in a cloud of bubbles. I couldn't see anything. I had one arm wrapped around the crocodile's head, holding its jaws closed, the other looped under its belly. The angry reptile rolled and twisted and wriggled, its sharp scales grinding like gravel against my bare chest. I had a weight advantage – the crocodile can't have weighed more than seventy pounds – but it was all muscle. And it was more at home in the water than on land. I was involved in a fight I couldn't win.

Several times as we rolled over and over, part of me came out of the water. Once I was even able to take a big gulp of air. And I kept bumping against the river's muddy bottom, which told me we were still in the shallows. It gave me a spark of hope. The next time my head came up, I drove down with both legs, planted my feet in the mud and heaved my body (and the crocodile) upright.

Success! I found myself knee-deep in the water, facing the river bank. I was holding the crocodile tight against my stomach in a bearhug. It was squirming like an eel and very heavy, but I had no illusions about what would happen if I let go while I was still in the water. I had to drag it ashore before releasing it. On dry land, I had a chance of getting away without being bitten.

How much of a chance, I'll never know. Before I had time to take a single step towards the shore, I heard something behind me and turned around.

Shishkebab! A massive brown-and-pink shape came plowing through the reeds like a living tsunami.

There was no escape. It was too late to run, too late to hide, and too late to duck for cover.

There was only one thing to do.

Summoning all my strength, I lifted the little crocodile chest-high and heaved it at the charging hippo.

SEEING RED

I don't know who won that contest. Crocodiles and hippos share the river, so maybe their unexpected meeting ended in a truce. Whatever happened, I didn't stick around long enough to find out. I was up the crocodile slide in a flash and running flat out away from the river.

I took one look over my shoulder, but the crocodile and the hippo were obscured by the river bank. The rest of the hippos were over near the other bank, eyeing the six hungry hyenas that prowled back and forth along the shore. The hyenas were eyeing me, but they couldn't cross the river because of the hippos. As long as I stayed on this side, I was safe.

But the road was on the other side.

What was that noise? Was I imagining it? I held my breath and listened. It sounded like – it definitely *was* – a vehicle. A long way off, but getting closer. I ran back the way I'd come. But only as far as the river. About twenty hippos and six hyenas watched me. No way was I going back across.

The noise grew steadily louder. A trail of dust rose through the trees on the other side of the river. When the vehicle finally came into view, roaring along the Marusha road, I waved my arms over my head and yelled at the top of my voice.

"Help! Help! Help!"

A second later I stopped yelling and lowered my arms. It was a battered gray Land Rover with a brown canvas canopy on the back. The white ivory hunter's thinly disguised threat came back to me: *A boy like you could wind up dead.*

"You wish!" I muttered, as the speeding vehicle disappeared around the side of the ridge.

But I didn't feel nearly as brave as I sounded. I was stuck on the wrong side of the river, and the only people who knew my whereabouts were a bunch of murderous poachers. They must have seen me.

I looked at my watch. It was 3:30 in the afternoon – two hours before the bus was due to arrive in Marusha. Two hours before anyone would know I was missing. Even if they came looking for me right away, there was no chance of them finding me before dark.

My bad eye had started throbbing again, and the other one wasn't much better. If I didn't get medical attention soon, I might lose my sight altogether. I couldn't just sit around and wait until help arrived. I had to help myself.

I stood there in my wet shorts and sneakers and tried to think what to do. Crossing the river again wasn't an option. Even if by some miracle I managed to get past the hippos a second time, the hyenas were on the other side.

Then I had a scary thought. *What was on this side?*

I was standing on the edge of a wide, yellow-grassed plain, dotted here and there with skinny, umbrella-shaped trees. A scatter of zebras, antelope and wildebeest grazed in the distance. It looked like a scene from a TV documentary about Africa. All that was missing were the lions. A shiver ran through me. Three large, pink-necked birds perched in one of the trees. Vultures. The heads of two more were visible above the long grass. Some creature lay dead under that tree, and I knew it hadn't died of old age.

Then I noticed something that made me forget about lions. The hills on the far side of the plain were shimmery and out of focus. But not so out of focus that I didn't see red.

I rubbed my blurry right eye and had a second look. Halfway up one of the hills, just below the edge of the forest, were two tiny red dots. Below them were a number of other dots – black ones, white ones and brown ones. Was it my imagination, or were some of the dots moving?

Suddenly, my heart began beating really fast. The black, white and brown dots were cattle. And the two red dots were people!

I started running.

MAN-EATER

On the bus, I'd overheard a conversation between two women in front of me. I hadn't meant to eavesdrop, but when they started talking about a man-eating leopard, I couldn't help listening. For the past year and a half, it had been terrorizing villagers in and around the Chui Hills – wherever that was. According to the women, the man-eater had killed five people.

Halfway across the plain, I saw something that brought their conversation back to mind. And gave me goose bumps all over. I skidded to a halt.

Shishkebab!

The big, spotted cat crouched in the yellow grass about a hundred and fifty yards away. Looking straight at me.

What was I going to do? I was in the middle of the plain, there was absolutely nowhere to hide, and anyway, the leopard had already seen me.

According to my big brother, the first rule in a tight situation is, *keep a cool head*. But Nathan had never come face to face with a leopard – especially not one that was quite possibly a man-eater. My palms were clammy, sweat dribbled down my face, and I was trembling uncontrollably. But I wasn't running away, which was the closest I could come to keeping a cool head.

Okay, Nathan, what next?

Second rule: *Figure out your options and how likely they are to succeed.*

There were two options that I could think of. The first was to turn around and start walking back towards the river. It was important to walk rather than run. If leopards were anything like dogs (and perhaps hyenas), the very worst thing I could do was run away from it. That would show I was afraid, and might encourage it to give chase.

My second option was more risky. I could bluff. I could pretend I wasn't the least bit scared of the leopard and walk right past it towards the hills.

Neither option seemed very likely to succeed, especially if the leopard was the man-eater. But I had to make a choice: the river or the hills?

The two red dots helped me make my decision.

It was the longest walk of my life. I felt like a condemned man on the way to the gallows – every step I took brought me that much closer to my doom.

I didn't walk directly towards the leopard – I wasn't that brave (or that stupid). Instead, I veered slightly to the left, so I would pass within fifty yards of it. That way, the leopard would be on my right, the same side as my good eye. Although "good" was hardly an accurate description – my right eye was stinging quite badly now, and the lids were beginning to swell closed like my bad eye. My vision was down to about thirty percent.

That's probably why, when the leopard jumped up, I thought it was charging.

When I said there were only two options, I left one out. There were actually three. But the third option was so radical that I'd dismissed it outright.

It's a strategy I use on little, yappy dogs that come rushing down their owners' driveways when

I'm delivering flyers. Instead of running away, I run towards them. Nine times out of ten, it stops them in their tracks.

And the tenth time? Well, I wear size 10 shoes …

But does my yappy dog strategy work with leopards? I still don't know. Because when I started running towards the tall, spotted cat, it was already racing off in the other direction. At about seventy miles per hour. It wasn't a leopard, it was a cheetah. Cheetahs aren't nearly as mean as leopards, and they never become man-eaters.

I stopped running just long enough to watch the cheetah race away, then staggered on towards the hills. I had a stitch, I was puffing like a steam engine, and I badly needed a drink, but I kept going. Herds of wildebeest, zebra and antelope watched me stumble past. Two huge marabou storks rose out of the long grass and flapped heavily into the sky. A family of warthogs trotted off in single file with their tails sticking straight up like flags. But I wasn't interested in the wildlife. With every step I took, the scene ahead of me grew clearer. The red dots were two Masai herders tending what looked to be a herd of goats – not cows as I'd originally thought. They had seen me now. When I waved, the smaller Masai waved back. It brought a lump to my throat. Unlike the ivory hunters, these people were friendly. They would help me. I was saved!

But my run across the plain had taken its toll. The continuous jolting had aggravated both my poisoned eyes, sending barbed-wire tendrils of pain shooting to every corner of my skull. It felt like my head was about to explode. *Ow! Ow! Ooooooow!*

At the bottom of the grassy slope, only a hundred yards from the two red-clad figures and their goats, I stumbled to a shaky standstill. I was delirious with a mixture of pain, dehydration and jet lag from the long flight from Australia. I couldn't take another step.

"Help me!" I gasped, clutching my head in both hands.

Then I fell flat on my face in the grass.

THE CHUI HILLS

"Jambo, mzungu."

I opened my blurry right eye to a narrow squint. Crouched over me were two boys. Both were younger than me and wore bright red Masai cloaks and sandals that seemed to be made out of car tires. One supported my head, the other held a long, thin pumpkin close to my mouth. I was hungry, but not *that* hungry.

"Water," I croaked, hoping they understood English.

The bigger boy smiled. He lifted the pumpkin so I could see it better. There was a hole at the skinny end, with beads of moisture sparkling around the edges. It wasn't a pumpkin, it was a water gourd.

"*Mzungu,* drink," he said.

I took a long, gulping swallow, nearly choking because I was lying down. It tasted awesome. "Thank you," I gasped. "Now, could you pour some on my eyes?"

Both boys looked puzzled.

"A snake – some sort of cobra – squirted me in the face."

The older boy said something in Swahili to his younger companion, then jumped to his feet and darted back up the hillside.

"Please pour some water in my eyes," I begged the little boy. "They're really hurting."

"Olki bring milk."

"I don't want milk, I want water," I said. "To wash my eyes."

He nodded solemnly. "Milk is good for wash eyes from sting."

Olki returned leading a scrawny brown-and-white animal on a short length of rope. At first I mistook it for a goat, but after I rubbed my eye I saw it was a weird, long-tailed sheep. The younger boy held its neck while Olki expertly milked it into an oval wooden bowl. When he'd collected enough, he wadded up a handful of the sheep's wool and used it to dab the warm, soothing liquid gently onto and around my eyes. Mostly he worked on my swollen left eye. The little boy held the lids open while Olki washed the eyeball with sheep's milk. When the pain was nearly gone, Olki tore a strip of fabric from the hem of his Masai cloak and tied it diagonally around my head so that it held the wad of milk-soaked wool in place over my left eye.

"Thank you," I said, sitting up. My left eye felt remarkably good beneath Olki's makeshift dressing, and the other one was nearly as good as new. "I'm sure glad I ran into you guys."

Olki looked solemn. "Milk make hurt go way, but do not make eye fixed. Only *mzungu* medicine will stop you go blind."

I shivered. "Where can I get *mzungu* medicine?"

"There is hospital at Marusha. You go there. Where is car?"

He thought I was old enough to drive. "I was on a bus," I said, and told them how I'd been left behind and everything that had happened since.

Olki reached inside his cloak and pulled out a blue

plastic watch that hung from his neck on a long loop of homemade string. "There is bus at eight o'clock. It will take you."

"How will I get back across the river?" I asked. "And what about the hyenas?"

The young Masai shepherd chewed his lip and stared off into the distance, deep in thought. "There is other road," he said finally. "This side of river. I will take you."

The two boys had a long conversation in Swahili, then Olki hurried away.

"Where's he going?" I asked the other boy, whose name I still didn't know.

"Olki get more milk. And spear."

Why does he need a spear? I wondered, but was afraid to ask.

While we waited for Olki to return, the younger boy and I introduced ourselves. His name was Momposhe and he was seven years old. Olki, his big brother, was ten. It surprised me that there were no adults with them.

"Aren't you scared of lions and leopards?"

"They not come close," Momposhe said. He gave me a gap-toothed smile. "Only in night. We stay at house, and sheeps and goats are safe inside big fence."

I glanced at the sun, already three-quarters of the way down the afternoon sky. "Do you live far from here?"

Momposhe pointed out a wispy blue column of smoke rising above the foothills about a mile away. "There our village," he said.

"Is there a road near it?" I asked hopefully.

He shook his brown, stubbly head. "Road on other side of hills."

I gazed up at the tall, heavily forested ridge towering over us – and had a really bad feeling.

"Momposhe, does this place have a name?"

He nodded. "Is call Chui Hills."

THE COLOR OF BLOOD

"Will he be all right?" I asked.

"Of course," said Olki. "Even sheep know way to village."

We had paused for a rest at the edge of the forest. Momposhe's tiny, half-naked figure herded the motley flock of sheep around the foot of the ridge far below us. I felt bad about leaving the younger brother on his own in the vast African landscape, and guilty for wearing his red cotton cloak. Momposhe had insisted I take it. "Now *mzungu* look like Masai," he'd said, knotting it across my left shoulder.

I didn't feel like a Masai – they were brave.

"Does eyes hurt, Sam?" Olki asked.

Gingerly, I touched my eye patch. "This one's getting a bit itchy."

Olki untied the bandage and poured more milk on the ball of wool. He had milked three more sheep before we set out, collecting it in a gourd which hung around his neck on a string. "Is hurting stop?" he asked, tying the dressing back in place.

"Yes, thank you," I said, looking around and blinking my other eye. A line of elephants was crossing the plain in the distance – coming from the direction of the river – but I couldn't make out if there was a calf in the group. "How far is the road?"

"One hour to walk."

I checked my watch. It was 4:45. "Is it forest all the way?"

Olki nodded. He hung the gourd back around his neck and picked up the spear. "We must hurry," he said, leading the way up into the trees.

The forest in the Chui Hills was different to that on the other side of the plain. It was more like a jungle. Huge, creeper-entangled trees formed a dense canopy overhead that completely blocked out the sky and cast an eerie green twilight. The forest floor was a tangle of vines, bushes, thorns and saplings, all competing for space with massive gray boulders and the trunks of the trees themselves. Olki and I sweated and struggled up a steep, narrow track. Our feet slipped, thorns plucked at our hair and clothing. Often we had to crawl under low branches or squeeze through narrow gaps between boulders. It was hard going. And very frightening.

Neither of us had mentioned the man-eater, but I was thinking about it every step of the way. It was on Olki's mind, too. He kept swiveling his head from side to side. The slightest rustle in the undergrowth caused him to freeze, his spear held at the ready. I wished I had a spear, too. Or better still, a .460 Weatherby Magnum. I'd come to Africa to help raise awareness about protecting endangered animals, but in the Chui Hills it was humans who were endangered.

Suddenly, a tiny deer – hardly bigger than a hare – came bursting out of a wild ginger bush and darted between us. Olki spun around so quickly that the spear nearly grazed my arm.

"Sorry," he said, grinning sheepishly as the dainty creature disappeared behind a huge, overgrown boulder. "Only *digidigi*."

A dik-dik, in English. I remembered seeing them on a David Attenborough show. They are the world's smallest antelope, and really cute. But cute animals didn't interest me right then. It was dangerous ones that were on my mind. Ones with spots. I could no longer keep my fear to myself.

"Olki, is it true that leopards sleep during the day?"

"Most times," he said softly.

I looked nervously right and left. We had stopped beneath a tree with fruit that resembled enormous gray sausages dangling out of its foliage on long, string-like stems. All around us were boulders and dense, shadowy forest. "What do you mean – *most* times?"

"If he hungry," Olki whispered, "leopard do not sleep."

Splat! Something warm and wet landed on my forehead just below my bandage. It felt like a large drop of water. I reached up and wiped it away.

Olki was staring at me, his eyes as big as Chupa Chups.

"What?" I asked.

He didn't say anything, simply pointed at the hand I'd used to wipe my forehead. I lowered my gaze. A long, damp smear ran across my palm. My vision was down to less than fifty percent, but I wasn't colorblind.

The smear was bright red – the color of blood.

64

LEOPARD

Olki and I stared at each other for a moment in stunned silence. Then we slowly raised our eyes to the branches of the sausage tree above our heads.

Shishkebab!

No wonder the dik-dik had been terrified. It must have known what was up there. That's why it had been hiding in the wild ginger bushes when we nearly stumbled over it.

Barely four feet above my head, another antelope lay wedged in the fork of two branches. It was a large, shaggy waterbuck. Stone dead. Something had killed it and dragged it up the tree.

There was only one animal in Africa capable of

doing that – a leopard.

Olki gripped my elbow and gently guided me around behind him. "We keep going up path, away from tree," he whispered. "Do not run, do not make noise, and do not stop till I say."

I was four years older than Olki and much bigger, but I didn't argue. I was a half-blind *mzungu* who had not set foot in Africa until twenty-four hours ago. Olki had been born and raised here. Plus, he had the spear. It was roughly six feet in length, with a long, tapered steel point. I could imagine what it would do to a leopard. But Olki was only ten years old. Too young to be a warrior.

Slowly, we backed up the track away from the tree. There were several deep claw marks carved into its bark. Sap dribbled out of them like sticky brown blood. The waterbuck seemed to watch us with its glassy, dead eyes. I couldn't see the leopard. It might have been anywhere in the maze of branches, leaves and weird, sausage-like fruit above our heads. I could feel its eyes on me as Olki and I backed slowly away from it up the narrow track. It was the creepiest sensation.

We reached the first of the boulders. Olki half-turned and silently mouthed a few words at me. I had no idea what he was saying, but Olki thought I understood. With a silent nod, he pushed past me around the boulder and set off up the steep, narrow track at a fast walk. I hurried to keep up, glancing nervously over my shoulder every two or three paces. I'd never felt more vulnerable. The leopard was behind us – that's where the danger lay – but Olki was walking in front. Plus, he had the spear. I had no way of defending myself. *Give me the spear, Olki,* I wanted to say. *If you're going to leave me to face the leopard, at least give me a fighting chance!*

But Olki didn't abandon me. He kept looking over his shoulder, too. And waiting for me if I started to fall behind. When I tripped over an exposed tree root, he came back and helped me to my feet.

"Does eyes hurt, Sam?" he asked.

"No, they're okay," I whispered. Who cared about my eyes? There was a leopard – possibly a man-eater – only three or four hundred yards down the track. Or closer, if it had left its tree and followed us.

Just then, a twig snapped in the undergrowth behind me. *Ohmygosh!* I nearly jumped out of my sneakers.

Olki grinned. "Only *nyani*," he said, pointing.

Through a gap in the foliage, I spied a young baboon intently picking berries off a low, bristly shrub. Two adults sat grooming each other under a larger bush a few yards beyond it. Looking around, I noticed at least a dozen more of the big olive-brown monkeys feeding in the undergrowth, or gazing down at us from rock ledges. Since leaving the sausage tree, I hadn't paid much attention to our surroundings. There were fewer trees here, and the sky was visible, although only a strip of it – we were in a deep, narrow gorge, bounded on both sides by hundred-foot walls of vertical rock. High above us, a large, bushy-maned baboon sat on a craggy outcrop, surveying his domain like the king of the castle.

"*Nyani* our friend," Olki said. "He tell us if leopard come."

The baboons seemed quite relaxed. The one that was the lookout would warn us if there was any danger. I let my breath out in a long, relieved sigh.

"I thought our number was up, Olki."

He seemed puzzled. "What number?"

"I thought we were dead. I could feel its eyes on us, couldn't you?"

Olki reached for the gourd of milk. He must have

thought I was talking about my own eyes. The left
one *was* starting to itch again. I sat down so Olki
could tend to it. But my mind was still on the leopard.

"Was it the man-eater?" I asked.

Olki didn't answer. He had stopped working on
my eye and was looking away from me. Milk dribbled
onto my elbow.

"Olki … ?"

"Shhh!"

I sat forward and listened, but I couldn't hear
anything. Olki knelt beside me, as still as a statue,
every muscle rigid. The ball of wool dangled forgotten
in his fingers. He was watching the big, male baboon
at the top of the cliff. *Olki, what is it?* I wanted to ask,
but the lookout baboon answered for him.

"*Whooh whooh whooh whooh!*" It barked in a loud,
deep staccato, like a kookaburra on steroids.

The troop's reaction was instantaneous. The
mother baboons grabbed their babies, and a wave of
panicked monkeys went scrambling up the vertical
rock face, screeching in alarm. Within seconds, Olki
and I were alone in the gorge.

Not quite alone. The lookout baboon was still
barking. "*Whooh whooh whooh whooh!*"

I didn't need Olki to interpret the warning. It had seen the leopard!

Olki hurriedly tied my dressing back in place. "We must run quick," he whispered, jumping to his feet and starting down the track. Back towards the sausage tree. Back the way we'd come!

Was he crazy?

"But the leopard's down there!" I called after him.

Olki stopped and shook his head. He pointed at the cliff top. All the baboons were barking. And every last one of them was looking *up* the gorge, not down it.

"*Nyani* watch leopard," Olki whispered.

I didn't argue. Olki obviously knew what he was talking about. The leopard must have left the sausage tree for some reason – perhaps to get water – and now it was returning to feed. Problem was, Olki and I were between it and its kill. And the cliffs looked too steep to climb.

We hurtled down the rocky, winding track at breakneck speed. Back the way we'd come. Back towards the sausage tree with the dead waterbuck in it.

A puzzling thought occurred to me. If the leopard went searching for water, wouldn't it go *down* the gorge rather than up?

There wasn't time to ask Olki about it. Because suddenly the track took a sharp, right-hand turn around a boulder, and there in front of us was the sausage tree.

The dead waterbuck was still wedged in its branches. And crouched over the waterbuck, looking directly at us, was a big yellow leopard.

DEAD BOYS RUNNING

We skidded to a standstill just short of the tree. The leopard bared its teeth at us and hissed – like a domestic cat, only louder. But one look at its massive, bloodstained canines, and you forgot all about domestic cats.

Olki was in front of me. I didn't see him throw the spear, but I heard it swish through the foliage. It cut down one of the big sausage-fruit and glanced harmlessly off a branch just above the leopard's head.

I don't blame Olki for throwing the spear. I probably would have done the same thing had our situations been reversed. But he missed the leopard, and now we were totally defenseless if it attacked.

It looked ready to attack. Straddling the partially devoured waterbuck, it put its ears back and snarled.

There was an answering snarl from behind us.

A tingly sensation ran up and down my spine. Seeing the leopard in the tree had driven all other thoughts from my head. I'd forgotten about the baboons and their warning that something was coming down the gorge behind us. Slowly, I turned my head.

There are several reasons why a leopard will become a man-eater. Usually it's old age, illness or an injury. The animal becomes too slow to hunt the antelopes, warthogs and monkeys that it normally eats, so it seeks out slower, less agile prey – sheep, goats, dogs, chickens ... and sometimes humans.

The leopard crouching in the wild ginger bushes no more than twenty feet away didn't look old, but it looked like something out of a nightmare. Sometime in the past it must have fought with a lion or a pack of hyenas and come off second best. One ear was gone and so was one eye, and there was no fur on half its head, just a vicious-looking scar. The scar was old, and a stubble of whiskers had grown back crookedly, but obviously the terrible injury had affected the animal's hunting ability. The mean glint in its remaining eye told me that this leopard – not the one in the tree – was the man-eater.

And not only did it look mean, it looked *hungry*.

Olki pressed against me. We stood back to back. Each of us faced a leopard. One was a man-eater, the other looked angry enough to do anything.

I weighed up our chances. They weren't good. Either leopard might kill us. It seemed unlikely that the one in the tree would come after us if we made a break for it, but the man-eater certainly would. How far would we get? Two paces? Five? We'd be dead boys running.

So far, the man-eater hadn't charged. We were sitting ducks, but for some reason it was hesitating. Was it because night hadn't fallen yet, and leopards prefer to hunt under the cover of darkness? Was it because Olki and I were together, and the man-eater felt slightly unsure about taking on two humans at the same time? Or was it because of the other leopard?

Leopards aren't social creatures like lions. They don't mix with others of their kind. Unless they're females rearing their cubs, they live and hunt on their own.

And they don't share their meals.

I took my eye off the man-eater just long enough to glance over my shoulder. The first leopard hadn't moved. It crouched over the dead waterbuck. Protecting it. From us. *And* from the other leopard.

Pressing back against Olki, I whispered, "Walk slowly towards the tree."

"But ... but ... the leopard!"

"Only two or three steps."

Back to back, we inched slowly towards the tree. Olki shuffled forwards, I edged backwards. I kept my single, blurry eye focused on the man-eater. It flicked the stump of its missing ear, otherwise it didn't move.

"Stop here," I whispered.

Near my feet lay the huge, sausage-shaped fruit that Olki had accidentally severed from the tree when he threw the spear. It was about twenty inches long and as thick as my arm. Without taking my eye off the man-eater, I slowly bent down and lifted the strange fruit by its long, trailing stem. It was heavy, just as I'd hoped – it must have weighed twelve or thirteen pounds.

"Duck your head," I whispered to Olki.

Gripping the long, fibrous stem firmly in both

hands, I swung the huge fruit back and forth a couple of times like a pendulum, getting the feel of it. Then I started twirling it above my head like an oversized slingshot, building up speed with every revolution.

Whoosh, whoosh, whoosh ...

I intended to hurl the sausage-fruit at the man-eater, but I twirled it one time too many, and the stem snapped off in my hands. Instead of going where I wanted, the huge gray missile went flying the other way. Over my shoulder and into the tree.

Whap!

It smashed into the waterbuck with such force that it knocked the dead antelope's hindquarters clean off the branch. Its back legs swung in the air. The leopard let out a deep-throated roar and sank its teeth and claws deep into the carcass to prevent it falling.

"Run!" hissed Olki, trying to push past me.

I grabbed his arm to stop him running straight into the jaws of the man-eater. With its single ear laid back, and its belly low to the ground, the hideous creature came creeping out of the ginger bushes.

"Other way," I whispered.

As the man-eater stalked menacingly towards us,

76

Olki and I backed down the path, closer and closer to the first leopard. We were nearly underneath it. It growled in warning, and the man-eater growled back. The first leopard growled again, but it was too busy struggling to keep the waterbuck on the branch to be a threat. I ducked to avoid the dead animal's dangling legs. Olki ducked, too.

Thirteen feet away, the man-eater tensed itself to spring.

Here goes nothing, I thought.

Reaching up, I wrapped my fingers around one of the waterbuck's cold, stiff legs.

The idea had formed in my mind when the two leopards started growling. The growls were a warning. The first leopard was warning all of us – not only Olki and me, but the man-eater as well – to stay away from its kill. And the man-eater was warning the other leopard to stay away from *us*.

What if neither leopard got what it wanted?

Gritting my teeth, I dragged the dead waterbuck down off the branch.

THE CATFIGHT TO END
ALL CATFIGHTS

My memory of the next few seconds is a blur. Several things happened at once.

I let go of the falling waterbuck and jumped out of the way.

Olki jumped in the opposite direction.

The waterbuck hit the ground in a cloud of dust, exactly where we'd been standing.

The leopard from the tree landed lightly on top of it.

The man-eater charged.

It was like a scene from *The Jungle Book*, except Mowgli had only one big cat to deal with. Olki and I had two. But – just as I'd hoped – two leopards is a deadly mix.

When the first leopard hit the ground, it was in a very bad mood. I'd tried to steal its kill, and that's about the worst thing you can do to a leopard. It knew I was to blame, but it was distracted by the other leopard – the man-eater – flying towards it with its claws out and its teeth bared.

The two leopards met head-on.

Leopards are the smallest of the big cats, but they're the most vicious fighters. When they turn on each other, it's the catfight to end all catfights. Roaring, snarling and hissing, they locked together in a flurry of raking claws and flashing teeth that spun back and forth across the track like a small yellow tornado. Dust and fur flew in all directions.

And so did Olki and I. The leopards were on the track, so we went bush. The plan was to put the maximum distance between us and the fighting leopards in the shortest time possible. But you can't move fast through the African bush – there are too many thorns. They tore at my clothing and snagged in my hair. After only a few feet, I was caught like a fly in a spider's web. I couldn't move.

I heard branches crackling close by and nearly jumped out of my skin. The man-eater! *Get a grip*, I told myself. The leopards were still fighting – noisily – on the track behind me.

"Stay still," Olki whispered in my ear. His nimble brown fingers went to work, unhooking Momposhe's tattered cloak from the thorns that held me prisoner. In ten seconds he had me free.

"Follow me, Sam."

On hands and knees, he led me along an animal tunnel similar to the one I'd used to escape the elephant. It looped around the boulder and joined the track about twenty yards up the gorge from the sausage tree. The boulder blocked our view of the leopards – and theirs of us – but their terrible bellows, snarls and roars echoed off the cliffs like the sounds of the final battle scene in *Lord of the Rings*. It made my hair stand on end.

Olki touched a finger to his lips to indicate silence and pointed up the track. This time he let me go in front. It was the third time we'd traveled along that stretch of track in fifteen minutes, and I knew the way. There was only one way – up the gorge. Away from the leopards.

The track was steep and rocky, but we flew up it like a pair of mountain goats. It's amazing how fast you can go when there are leopards behind you.

But leopards are faster.

"Whooh whooh whooh whooh!"

"Sam, wait!" Olki hissed, behind me.

I stopped and turned around. "What is it?"

Instead of saying anything, Olki pointed. High on its rocky outcrop sat the same big, bushy-maned baboon that had warned us about the man-eater earlier. Now it was barking again. Only this time it was looking *down* the gorge.

And then it registered. I could no longer hear the leopards fighting. From the baboon's behavior, it was clear that one of the leopards was making its way up the gorge. In our direction. And it didn't take a genius to figure out which one.

"Quick, quick!" urged Olki. He led me off the track, through the shrubs where we'd seen the baboons feeding earlier, and straight to the gorge's sheer rock wall.

"Olki, what are you *doing*?" I whispered. "The man-eater's coming!"

He was walking along the cliff base, gazing upwards. "We get far from path. Leopard too fast."

"Won't it smell us?"

Olki stopped next to a tall, vertical split in the rock face. It was roughly three feet wide by six feet deep and ran halfway up the cliff. A spindly tree grew out of the crevice about forty feet above our heads. It was supported by long, outflung roots that clung to the rock like the tentacles of an octopus.

"Climb up," Olki said.

It was our only hope. Leopards can climb trees, but they can't scale cliffs.

Olki went first. Slipping into the fissure, he braced his back against one side and his sandals against the other. Then, pushing hard with his flattened hands on the rock behind him and inching one foot at a time up the rock in front, he began "walking" slowly up the vertical rock chimney. As soon as he was high enough, I slid into the narrow space underneath him and began following his example. It was hard work and painfully slow. We had to creep up the crevice a half-inch at a time. One slip, and we'd fall all the way back down.

When we were more than halfway to the tree, the lookout baboon started shrieking hysterically. It sounded terrified. The man-eater must be close. Even so, I wasn't expecting what happened next.

There was a loud, deep cough, followed by a scratching noise right below me. I looked down.

Shishkebab! My heart nearly stopped. The man-eater was *right there!* Less than three feet away. Clinging to the wall of the rock chimney with its deadly, scimitar claws.

I froze. *Leopards can't climb cliffs*, I told myself. It must have jumped up from the ground thirteen feet below. It could hold on, but it couldn't come any closer. Its eye was greenish-yellow, the pupil large in the fading daylight, its gaze almost hypnotic – the look of a predator sizing up its prey. But I was just out of its reach, and we both knew it. The man-eater bared its huge, saber-like canines and growled, a truly terrifying sound at such close quarters. I got a whiff of its warm, sour breath. Then it started slipping. Its claws made a tearing noise, carving parallel white tracks in the brown rock as it slid slowly down and away from me. With a final bellow of frustration, the man-eater sprang away from the cliff, twisting its body around in midair and landing lightly on all fours like a cat.

No sooner had it hit the ground than the leopard ran in a half-circle, bunched its muscular hindquarters like springs and jumped again. This time it only made it twelve feet up the rock face before it slid scratchily back down.

"Climb more high, Sam!" Olki hissed, from above me. He had nearly reached the sprawling roots of the tree. "Quick, quick!"

It shook me out of my trance. With trembling arms and legs, I resumed my painstakingly slow passage up the rock chimney. Every fiber of my being screamed at me to take Olki's advice (*Quick, quick!*), but I forced myself not to hurry. I couldn't afford to slip. The man-eater jumped three more times, but with each attempt I was further from its reach. Finally, it gave up and disappeared into the bushes, limping slightly – either from its repeated falls, or from its fight with the other leopard.

It wasn't until I'd reached the tree's roots and scrambled up onto its narrow sloping trunk that I began to feel safe. But we weren't out of danger yet. Far from it. There was still a lot of climbing to do. About thirteen feet above us was a ledge. It zigzagged the rest of the way up the cliff like a stairway. But to reach it we had to climb almost to the top of the tree. The tree sloped out from the cliff, and our weight made it slope even further. Its skinny trunk began to bend and creak as Olki and I clambered up through the branches. I worried it might snap, or its roots might break free of their precarious hold on the rock face.

"You go first," I whispered to Olki.

I worked my way back down to the base of the tree, where its trunk grew out of the rock. Keeping a wary eye out for the man-eater, I waited while Olki scrambled safely onto the ledge. Then I started climbing back up the tree.

I was much heavier than Olki. By the time I drew level with him, the tree was bending away from the cliff at a scary angle. I couldn't reach the ledge. Olki lay flat on his belly and stretched out one hand. I rocked the tree towards him and made a wild grab. Our fingers locked together. Breathing heavily, Olki pulled me slowly towards him. The tree bent like a spring. When I seemed to be close enough, I let go of the tree with my other hand and swung it across the gap. But it was difficult to judge distances with only one eye, and my hand missed the ledge. Then Olki's fingers slipped from my grasp. If it wasn't for my legs wrapped around the tree trunk, I would have fallen. I swayed sickeningly back and forth, the forest floor far below. Before I could lose my nerve, I made another desperate lunge. Olki stretched across with his free hand and grabbed my wrist. Now I was nearly horizontal across the gap, the tree pulling me one way, and Olki pulling the other.

"I slip!" gasped Olki.

The tree was winning the tug-of-war, dragging me, inch by inch, away from the ledge. And dragging Olki, inch by inch, *off* the ledge. I couldn't let go with my legs because they were supporting most of my weight. But if I *didn't* let go, I was going to pull Olki off his rocky perch.

Below us, somewhere deep in the shadowy gorge, the man-eater made a series of low, coughing grunts. The sound echoed eerily around the cliffs and started the lookout baboon screeching again. I knew the leopard was watching us. Waiting for us to fall. Already it had killed five people. That was five people too many. No way were Olki and I going to be numbers six and seven.

"Push me," I said.

Olki's eyes grew big. *"What?"*

"Push me back towards the tree."

He hesitated for two seconds. Long enough for the tug of the branch to drag him another half-inch off the ledge. A tiny avalanche of sand and pebbles tumbled down the vertical cliff face below us.

"Do it!" I yelled. "On the count of three. One … two … three … *push!*"

Olki must have thought I was crazy, but my raised voice shook him into action. He pushed and let go. I flew backwards. Twisting my body like a corkscrew, I grabbed the tree trunk as it sprung away from the cliff. It swayed gut-churningly out over the gorge, with me attached. *Please don't snap*, I prayed, throwing my weight outwards to maximize the swing. The tree bent and bent, much further than I'd anticipated. For a horrifying moment I was dangling nearly upside down. Wood creaked. A shower of small stones clattered down from the tree's straining roots. Then, with a squealing groan, the branch began to straighten. I felt myself rising, slowly at first, then faster, as the branch flicked up in a big, swishing arc that lifted me out of the gorge and catapulted me straight at the cliff.

For a second I was flying.
Crunch!

I didn't make it all the way onto the ledge. Only my top half did. The lower half, my hips and legs, slammed into the rock face. I tried to cushion the impact with my hands, but my midriff hit the ledge full force, and all the wind was knocked out of me. For a moment I was paralyzed, unable to breathe, unable to move. I would have fallen to my death had Olki not been there to drag me up onto the narrow, rocky shelf.

"You nearly falled," he said.

Lying flat on my back, dazed, bruised and fighting to regain my breath, I nodded in silent agreement. I couldn't talk.

So when I saw a sudden movement behind him, all I could do was point.

"What – " Olki began to ask, turning his head.

But it was too late.

SELF-DEFENSE

I've seen a lot of TV shows about wildlife in Africa, and mostly they reckon baboons aren't dangerous. It's only the semi-wild ones that can be a problem, especially around popular tourist spots where people feed them. Olki and I weren't in a tourist spot, nor did we have any food to attract the baboons. But there's another reason why a normally non-aggressive animal will attack a human – fear. Either fear for its young, as in the case of the mother elephant, or fear for its life.

The baboon that attacked Olki and me was in fear for its life – not from us, but from the leopard. Baboons are wary of humans, but they're *terrified* of leopards. That's why it was hiding in a narrow fissure in the rock face at the rear of the ledge. When Olki first appeared outside its hiding place, the baboon must have crouched there hoping not to be seen. But then I came crashing into view and lay there gasping. Now there were two humans blocking its escape route. The baboon felt trapped. It knew the leopard was nearby, and it panicked.

Olki didn't see it coming. He'd only half-turned his head when the baboon landed on his shoulders. It was an adolescent male, only three-quarters grown, but even so, it must have weighed sixty-five pounds. Olki collapsed under its weight. It was lucky he did because the big, dog-faced monkey aimed a vicious bite at the side of his head, missing his ear by less than an inch when Olki pitched forward.

Both of them fell on top of me. Screeching like a creature from a horror movie, the baboon clawed at Olki's back, ripping his cloak half-off him. I got one arm free and knocked it sideways. It did a backwards somersault and landed in a knot of hairy limbs, like a flicked huntsman spider. Instantly, it untangled itself and spun around.

Baring its massive yellow teeth, the baboon grunted like a pig and leapt straight for my head.

Olki was still lying on top of me; I couldn't get out of the way. The baboon came at me with its mouth wide-open, its long, clawed fingers reaching for my neck. I put up a left-hand block, then dragged my right arm free and gave the baboon a spearhand jab to the throat. It's an illegal move in karate, but this was self-defense – the baboon would have bitten my face off otherwise. I was still winded and didn't put much force into the blow, but it was enough to throw my attacker off balance. Olki did the rest. Jackknifing his body, he whipped his legs around and kicked the baboon off the ledge. With a shriek of terror, it fell into the tree below, grabbing hold with one foot and one hand to stop itself plunging all the way into the gorge.

Olki helped me to my feet. My stomach felt bruised where I'd smashed into the ledge, and my bandaged eye throbbed.

"Can you walk?" Olki asked.

"Yeah," I wheezed. It hurt to talk. "Will it attack us again?"

Olki glanced at the baboon eyeing us warily from the tree. "No. He scared of leopard. Quick, we go up."

I followed Olki up the narrow, zigzagging ledge,

casting frequent looks over my shoulder. When we were halfway up, the baboon leapt across from the tree and came padding up the ledge on all fours. I nearly started to panic, then I saw that it was deliberately hanging back, waiting for us to reach the top first. Olki was right – the baboon was just as scared as we were. It kept looking over its shoulder. Back into the gorge.

"Olki," I said softly. "Can the leopard … ?"

"Shhh!" he whispered, dropping into a crouch.

I crouched, too, although I didn't know why. Had Olki seen something? We were on a wide, rocky shelf that stretched along the lip of the gorge. Before us stood a shadowy wall of forest. It looked dark and forbidding in the fading light of late afternoon. My skin prickled. This was Africa. Anything could be hiding among those trees: lions, rhinos, hyenas, *leopards*.

There was a shuffling noise behind me. I spun around. The baboon came scampering up over the skyline. He was looking the other way, back over his shoulder, and was about to run into us.

"Whoa, boy!" I cried, raising my hands in a double block.

The baboon saw us at the last moment and let

out a grunt of surprise. It was too late to stop, so it jumped clear over our heads and disappeared into the forest at a flat-out run.

Olki raised his eyebrows. "*Nyani* scared," he said.

"*It's* scared?" I joked, showing him my trembling hands. "Look at me! I'm shaking like a – "

"Shhh!" Olki tilted his head, listening.

That was when I realized how silent it was. No sound came from the forest – not a bird call, not a rustling leaf, not the rasp of a cricket. Olki and I might have been the only living things for a hundred miles. I wished we were! But I was out of luck.

Olki drew in his breath with a sharp hiss. I looked at him. Instead of saying anything, he pointed.

About three hundred yards down the gorge was an old, overgrown rock fall. The setting sun cast it in deep shadow, and my vision was down to thirty percent, but when I focused my good eye and concentrated, I saw a pale, cat-like shape working its way stealthily up over the boulders towards the top of the gorge.

Olki rose to his feet.

"How fast can run, Sam?" he asked.

AFRICA'S MOST DANGEROUS

It was a deadly game of cat and mouse. Olki and I were the mice. We had a head start of two or three minutes. That might sound like a lot, until you remember that the cat was a man-eating leopard.

To my mind, there was only one way to go: along the lip of the gorge, *away* from the man-eater. But Olki had other ideas. Turning his back on the gorge, he led me directly into the forest. What was he thinking? The leopard would be right at home in the forest; it could move through the tangled undergrowth with ease, whereas Olki and I had to push and struggle every step of the way.

Two things worked in our favor. Firstly, we were

going downhill. And secondly, there weren't any thorns. Even so, it was slow, slow, *slow!*

"Where are we going?" I puffed.

"To find stream," Olki whispered, over his shoulder.

Was he kidding? There was a man-eater chasing us! "Olki, we can get a drink later," I said.

"Not for drink," he whispered, "for escape from leopard."

"How can we escape in a stream?"

"It not smell in water," whispered Olki.

I was about to congratulate Olki on his quick thinking, when we came charging out of the trees into a small, reedy swamp, hidden in a pocket in the hills.

And skidded to a halt.

The buffalo stood knee-deep in the swamp about twenty-five yards out from the shore. Two slimy green reeds dangled half-eaten from the corners of its mouth. Muddy water fell, *drip, drip, drip,* from its lower jaw. If an animal could look grumpy at having its meal interrupted, that was the buffalo's expression. It raised its big, ugly head, put its ears back and snorted.

The Cape buffalo is one of the "Big Five" wild animals that every tourist going to Africa wants to see. The other four are the lion, the leopard, the elephant and the rhino. They are called the Big Five because back in the days when people went on safari with guns rather than cameras, these five animals were considered Africa's most dangerous. Sometimes it was the hunter who ended up dead.

People are often surprised that the Cape buffalo is included in the Big Five. But if they met one face to face, they wouldn't be surprised at all.

Imagine the biggest bull you've ever seen. Now make it a foot and a half bigger – in all directions – and twice as heavy. Give it a pair of horns wider than your outstretched arms and as thick as mallee roots. Lastly, give it the personality of a pit bull terrier. That's a Cape buffalo.

"Go back to trees," Olki said softly.

I didn't need to be told twice. I'd been attacked by more than my fair share of animals in my short life, and I knew the warning signs.

Together, Olki and I started edging backwards through the slippery mud towards the safety of the forest. But we both knew it wasn't safe. Behind us, only a few hundred yards further up the ridge, a baboon started barking its now-familiar warning. I cast a nervous glance over my shoulder. The man-eater was coming.

And so was the buffalo. From the other direction. The moment I looked away, it charged.

"Climb tree!" yelled Olki, making a run for it.

One look at the buffalo plowing towards us, and I was hot on Olki's heels. There was an obvious tree to climb. Standing at the edge of the forest, its trunk was taller and thicker than those around it and had a series of out-flung branches like the rungs of a ladder. But they started nearly nine feet above the ground. Olki leapt up and grabbed one, swinging his small, wiry body up like a gymnast. I wasn't so skilful. Because of my impaired eyesight, I misjudged the distance and jumped too high. Instead of wrapping my fingers around the branch, I whacked it with my wrists and fell back down.

Luckily, I landed on my feet. But the buffalo was just behind me. I could hear it coming. I could feel it coming. The ground shook. The air shook. I jumped again. This time I got it right. My fingers found the branch. The moment I grabbed hold, I started bringing my legs up and forwards, swinging my body ...

Whump!

I didn't get totally clear. When the buffalo slammed into the tree, the trailing edge of my cloak got caught on one of its horns. The other end was still looped around my neck and knotted over my left shoulder. I couldn't undo the knot because I didn't have any free hands. In desperation, I jackknifed my body and wrapped my legs around the branch. Now I was dangling under the branch like a sloth. The buffalo was just below me. It snorted and shook its huge head, jerking me from side to side like an upside-down puppet. I was helpless. I couldn't do anything to save myself. All the buffalo had to do was pull, and I'd fall out of the tree. But buffalos aren't very bright. Instead of pulling, it tried to head-butt me. Luckily, buffalos can't jump. I was just out of its reach.

"Hold on, Sam," whispered a voice, just above me. Olki lowered himself onto the branch and began untying the knot that secured the cloak around my neck.

But he only got it half-undone. Suddenly, the buffalo let out a deafening bellow and charged away from the tree. It tore me from the branch. I landed on the animal's broad, mud-caked shoulders, bounced a couple of times, then flipped high into the air. The next moment I was under the buffalo's head, being dragged along the ground, my legs and feet trailing between its thrashing hooves. I grabbed at my cloak where it looped around my neck, to stop myself being strangled. The super-sized bull let out another angry bellow and jerked its head up and sideways, swinging me out from underneath it.

For a second I was completely upside down. I glimpsed a flash of yellow fur and heard a yowl of pain, but everything was spinning, and I couldn't figure out what was going on. Somehow I landed on my feet, with my right shoulder nearly touching the buffalo's eye. But its gaze wasn't directed at me, it was looking straight ahead. I swiveled my own eye sideways.

Shishkebab!

No more than three paces away, crouched low to the muddy ground, was the man-eater.

The scar-faced leopard wasn't looking at me, it was watching the buffalo. Its single ear was laid back flat against its head, and its teeth were bared in a silent, threatening snarl. But it looked nervous. Its fur was matted and disheveled, and there was a smear of fresh, wet mud across its spotted back and flanks. Leopards don't like being wet and they never roll in mud. It must have been tossed by the buffalo when the huge animal swung its head. Few animals are capable of killing a leopard, but the Cape buffalo is one of them. Mature bulls weigh twenty times more than leopards, and their horns are formidable weapons. And they don't like leopards. The man-eater had come looking for Olki and me, and unwittingly blundered into the territory of its arch-enemy.

The buffalo stamped one massive hoof in the mud and snorted. That was enough for the man-eater. It had already been tossed once. With a frustrated hiss, it turned and went bounding off into the undergrowth. The buffalo stared at the spot where it had disappeared for a moment, then swiveled its eye around to look at me.

And as its eye moved, so did its head, swinging those massive, curved horns in a vicious left hook that would have KO'd a rhinoceros.

Whoosh!

TEMBO!

In the six or eight seconds that had passed while the buffalo's attention was focused on the leopard, my fingers had been busy. I'd finished untying the knot on my left shoulder. When the buffalo took a swipe at me – *whoosh!* – I hurled myself backwards and flipped the free end of my cloak up over its head.

Now the buffalo couldn't see. The cloak was covering its eyes. It went crazy. Bellowing, snorting and tossing its head, it began charging blindly in circles, kicking its back legs high in the air like a massive rodeo bull. I backed quickly out of the danger zone, keeping a wary lookout for the man-eater and trying to get my bearings. I spotted the tree where I'd left Olki, but he wasn't in it.

"Sam!" he hissed, behind me. He was wading out into the swamp. "Come quick, quick!"

I remembered what he'd said about the leopard not being able to track us in water, but going into the swamp seemed like a very bad idea. There might be hippos, crocodiles, other buffalos. And our buffalo was bound to get the cloak off its head before too long. Still, we didn't have a lot of choices. It was either the swamp (hippos, crocodiles, buffalos) or the forest (man-eater). I followed Olki into the muddy brown water.

The swamp wasn't large, about the size of a soccer field, and was only waist deep. Swirling clouds of mosquitoes buzzed around our heads as we pushed through the reeds and the mud and the tangled mats of water hyacinth, all the way to the other side.

Now what? I wondered, glancing nervously back the way we'd come. The reeds hid the buffalo from view, but I could hear it sloshing around in the water not very far away. It seemed to be coming in our direction.

"We've got to get out of here," I whispered, flicking a leech off my naked belly. "The leopard's probably miles away by now."

Olki didn't seem to be listening. He waded slowly ahead of me, his keen eyes searching the shore. For what, I had no idea.

But I soon found out.

"Go this way," Olki hissed, parting the reeds to reveal the mouth of a small, trickling stream that fed into the swamp from the steep, forested hills above us.

It was our escape route.

We walked single file up the stream, staying in the water every step of the way and being very careful not to brush against any overhanging leaves or branches and leave our scent on them. Sometimes we had to wriggle under obstacles on our bellies, like platypuses. We got covered in mud and were sopping wet from head to toe. But it was vital that we didn't leave a trail for the man-eater to follow. I had come to trust Olki's judgment, and he said the leopard wouldn't give up simply because the buffalo had attacked it.

"He too hungry," Olki whispered.

My skin prickled. There was a hungry man-eater on the prowl, and night was falling. I nervously surveyed our surroundings. We were in a steep, narrow valley, with thick forest on all sides. You couldn't see more than fifteen or twenty feet in any direction.

"Is it far to the road?" I asked.

Olki shrugged.

I frowned at him. "Are we lost?"

He chewed his lower lip. I saw the guilt and fear in his eyes. "I am sorry, Sam," he whispered.

"It's not your fault," I said, remembering that he was only ten years old. He had risked his life by coming into the Chui Hills. And he'd done it for me – because I needed to go to the hospital. My eyes still felt better than they had before Olki's milk treatment, but there was a deep, throbbing ache behind the bandaged one that told me it was far from cured. I looked at my watch. 6:15 p.m. We still had nearly two hours to catch the bus.

"I think we should get out of this valley," I said. "We need to get to higher ground so we can see where we are."

"But … leopard?" whispered Olki.

"We'll have to take the risk. If we keep following the stream, we're going to run out of daylight."

And if we ran out of daylight while still lost in the Chui Hills, our fate was sealed.

Olki said the water looked okay, so we had a drink,

and I rinsed my good eye. Then we started up the side of the valley. It was steep and heavily overgrown, and we were exhausted, but when your life is on the line you find hidden reserves of energy.

The climb took about fifteen minutes. At the top, we staggered out of the trees onto a well-used game trail that followed the spine of a long, sloping ridge. In one direction it zigzagged down through the forest towards the wide, grassy plain – deep in shadow now – that I'd crossed earlier in the afternoon. In the other direction, the trail wound its way up through the forest towards a broad, tree-lined summit, no more than half a mile away.

"Is that the top of Chui Hills?" I asked.

Olki nodded. "Road other side. Not far."

We passed several large mounds of elephant dung as we hurried up the game trail. Some looked quite fresh. But my thoughts were mostly concerned with the man-eater and whether or not we'd outsmarted it. The few clothes I was wearing – shorts, socks, sneakers – were sopping wet from our journey up the stream. And my bandaged eye had started bothering me again. Every five or ten seconds there would be a sudden, sharp stab of pain, like someone sticking a needle into my eyeball.

But Olki had dropped the gourd of milk sometime during our flight. I remembered his warning that if I didn't get medical attention that night, I might end up permanently blind.

Finally, we reached the summit and paused to catch our breath. The first pale stars of evening winked down through the trees. Night was falling. But Olki reckoned it wasn't far to the road. All we had to do was follow the trail. And it was all downhill. For the first time, it felt like we were actually going to make it.

Then a baboon broke the silence. *"Whooh whooh whooh whooh!"*

It sounded close.

Olki and I exchanged a fearful look – a look that said, *man-eater!* – and started to run.

A human can't outrun a leopard. If the man-eater had found our scent, Olki and I could have saved our energy. It would have been better to climb a tree and try to fend it off with sharp sticks. But when there's a man-eater behind you and a road somewhere ahead, you don't think logically. Every atom of your being tells you to run.

We hadn't gone far – perhaps two hundred

yards – when I heard Olki say something. But he was puffing like a steam train, and I didn't catch what it was. And I was too puffed myself to ask him to repeat it. I was putting all my concentration into seeing where I was going. It was almost fully dark now, and I was down to only one eye – I had to focus really hard on the bumpy trail just ahead of my running feet, otherwise I'd go head over heels.

Olki repeated what he'd said, louder this time. We'd been running side by side, but suddenly his voice came from behind me. I slowed down and glanced over my shoulder. He had stopped and was standing in the middle of the trail, pointing at me. It was too dark to see the expression on his face, but when he repeated himself again, his voice sounded urgent.

"Tembo!"

Finally, I got it. Elephant. And I realized Olki wasn't pointing at me, he was pointing past me.

I turned to look.

Holy guacamole!

WE MEET AGAIN

The elephant towered over me, an enormous black silhouette standing in the middle of the trail. It was no more than ten feet from where I'd skidded to a stop.

I stood frozen in shock. It felt like déjà vu – a nightmare come back to haunt me. Dangling from one of the elephant's tusks was a pale strip of torn fabric.

She rumbled, as if to say, *we meet again*.

I was dead meat. Elephants are supposed to have good memories, and it was only a couple of hours since our last meeting – when I'd slapped her calf, swung from her tail and tied my shirt around her trunk. They weren't good memories. She had a score to settle.

But she didn't move. Cautiously, I backed away from her up the trail. Instead of charging, the elephant flapped her ears and made a soft, echoey sound deep in her trunk.

Olki grabbed my arm. "Follow me," he whispered, leading me into the trees.

We took a wide detour through the shadowy forest and rejoined the trail about twenty yards past the elephant. I wished we'd gone further. She was much too close for comfort. I knew how fast she could run.

"It's the same one that nearly killed me this afternoon," I gasped, setting off down the trail as fast as I dared in the rapidly failing light.

Olki's eyesight was three times as good as mine, and he had no trouble keeping up. "Do not worry," he said. "She not leave baby."

"I didn't see a baby."

"Under big tree beside mother. One leg tied with wire."

I came puffing to a standstill. *"What?"*

Olki stopped, too. "Baby *tembo* caught in hunter trap. Mother stay with it."

I peered back up the trail. All I could see with my one blurry eye was the huge black blob of the mother. "Why do they catch baby elephants?"

"Not want babies," whispered Olki. "Bad luck for baby to step in wire. Hunters catch big *tembo* for tusk."

Suddenly, I understood. Ivory hunters. A chill ran up and down my spine. "We have to go back and save them."

"No, Sam, cannot save," said Olki, lowering his voice. "Leopard coming."

He was right. We had to save ourselves. But it made me sick to think of the mother elephant staying with her snared calf until the poachers came and killed her in cold blood. They would probably kill the baby, too.

Olki drew in his breath. "Listen. Hear bus."

I paused for a moment. Yes! I could hear it, too – the distant rumble of a vehicle.

Without waiting for a message from my brain, my legs started running, carrying me down the trail towards the road. At least, I trusted that was where we were going. It was fully dark now. All I could see was the pale, flapping shape of Olki's cloak just ahead of me. I locked on that and ran.

And ran and ran and ran.

When Olki suddenly slowed down, I wasn't ready

for it. I kept running – straight into his back. Both of us sprawled to the ground.

"Sorry," I gasped, rolling off him. "Are you okay?"

Olki raised his head and screwed up his eyes. His face was damp with sweat, and there were patches of red dust like clown's makeup on his nose, chin and cheeks. I felt confused. Not about the patches of dust, but because I could see him. There was light on his face, a bright light – bright enough to make him squint. I turned my head and was nearly blinded.

A pair of headlights came bumping up the trail towards us.

I jumped to my feet and rushed towards the lights, waving my hands in the air and yelling, *"Stop, stop, stop!"*

The vehicle halted in the middle of the trail, and its engine slowed to an idle. I couldn't see a thing, just the two blinding circles of light. A door creaked open.

"Well, well, well," said a voice that started a hundred warning bells jangling inside my head. "We meet again."

21

FIRING SQUAD

My eyesight might not have been good, but there was nothing wrong with my brain. It was the ivory hunter I'd met that afternoon on the Marusha road. He and his two partners-in-crime must have been the ones responsible for setting the snare that had captured the baby elephant. Now they were coming back to check if they'd caught anything.

I had to stop them.

Clutching my bandaged head, I let out a loud groan and collapsed in the middle of the trail.

"Hey, Aussie," the white poacher called, "can you hear me?"

Did it look like I could hear him? I pretended to be

unconscious.

A second door creaked open, and I heard the two Africans getting out. The three men had a conversation in Swahili. I expected Olki to join in – or at least to come and see if I was okay – but he didn't. It seemed strange that the poachers were ignoring him. Footsteps came rustling towards me. A heavy boot prodded my shoulder.

"Hey, Aussie."

I lay still. Everything depended on them thinking I was unconscious. The poacher prodded me again, harder this time. It hurt. I gritted my teeth and ordered myself not to move. The elephants' lives depended on it. Possibly even *my* life depended on it. These were dangerous men.

There was another conversation in Swahili. The white man sounded angry. I think he wanted to drag me to the side of the trail and leave me there. But the two Africans were arguing with him. The word *chui* was repeated several times. Leopard. A shiver ran through me. The man-eater could be anywhere in the surrounding forest. Watching us. Watching *me*. Waiting for the Land Rover to drive away, and then ...

I made a decision. If the poachers decided to leave

me, I would stop pretending to be unconscious and beg them to take me with them.

Luckily, that wasn't necessary. Muttering in the grumpy tone of someone who'd lost an argument, the white man went stomping off towards the Land Rover. The two Africans picked me up. One held me under the armpits, the other had my legs. I tried to stay limp. They carried me around to the back of the Land Rover and set me on the ground, just below the puttering exhaust pipe. The fumes were suffocating, but I didn't dare turn my head away. Holding my breath, I heard the two Africans unclipping a series of press studs, then they picked me up and heaved me into the Land Rover's canvas-covered rear section. I landed on a lumpy tarp and lay motionless while they clipped the canvas closed behind me.

Only when the doors slammed, and the Land Rover jolted into motion, did I dare open my eye. It was pitch black; I might as well have left it closed. But my trick had worked – I'd fooled the poachers into thinking I was unconscious.

Now what? I wondered, as we bounced up the bumpy trail. I realized that the poachers were probably still going to check their snare. I hadn't saved the elephants at all, I'd just delayed their deaths by two or three minutes.

And what had happened to Olki?

Pop, pop, pop!

The noise came from right next to my head. It was the press studs coming undone. I shuffled quickly away. The canvas parted, and a wedge of starry sky appeared. Silhouetted against the Milky Way was a small, crouched figure.

"Olki?" I whispered.

He was balanced on the Land Rover's spare wheel, swaying back and forth like a yachtsman in heavy seas as the four-wheel drive lurched and bounced.

"You okay, Sam?" he asked.

"I'm fine. I was just pretending to be sick to fool the hunters."

Olki's teeth flashed in the starlight. "Good trick," he said. "They do not see me in dark. I hide in trees, then jump on truck."

I helped him climb in. The heavy canvas flapped closed behind him, and once more it was pitch dark. Olki crouched next to me, his warm breath tickling my bare shoulder. The Land Rover lurched and swayed. Whatever was under the tarp – it felt like firewood – rolled back and forth beneath us, making it very uncomfortable to lie on. I crawled blindly forward, feeling with my hands for somewhere more stable, and nearly collided with a big, iron tool box. I wriggled on top of it, wedging my back into the corner where the canvas side of the truck met the rear of the cab. It was weird to think that the three poachers were just through that connecting wall, with only the canvas and an inch of sheet metal separating us.

Olki came scrambling in my direction. I couldn't see anything, but I heard the wood shifting and clunking underneath him. Just as he reached me, the Land Rover jolted to an abrupt stop, throwing him against me. His weight pressed my face into the connecting wall. My bandaged eye saw stars. But my other eye, the one squashed against the canvas, saw something else: a strip of pale yellow light.

I'd been wrong about what separated me and Olki from the poachers. It wasn't canvas and sheet metal, it was canvas and glass. There was a window at the rear of the cab, hidden behind a flap in the canvas.

Using one finger, I carefully moved the flap to the side. Now Olki and I could see into the cab. The two Africans were getting out one door, and the white man was getting out the other. He dragged his big elephant gun behind him. I lifted the flap a bit higher, until we had a view out through the windshield. I saw immediately why we'd stopped.

Forty yards up the trail, illuminated by a powerful spotlight mounted somewhere on top of the Land Rover, stood the mother and baby elephant. I could see a wire noose wrapped around one of the calf's back legs. The other end was secured to the trunk of a huge mahogany tree growing at the edge of the trail. Both elephants stood silently staring at us. Their eyes had a wet glisten in the light, like tears.

They looked just like two condemned prisoners facing a firing squad.

THE CUNNING SNAKE

"I'm going to stop them," I said, crawling back across the lumpy tarp towards the opening at the rear of the Land Rover.

"They have gun," whispered Olki.

I didn't care. I'd just realized what was under the tarp – not firewood, *elephant tusks*. When I vaulted out of the back of the Land Rover, I felt angry enough to take on all three poachers at once. With my bare hands.

Even though I learn karate – and technically my hands are weapons – it would have been suicide. One half-blind boy versus three grown men, one of whom was packing a .460 Weatherby Magnum. Go figure.

"Look what I find," whispered Olki, passing me an axe from the Land Rover's pitch-black interior. Then he clambered out over the spare wheel carrying a small, collapsible shovel, which he proceeded to twirl above his head in a very dangerous manner. "We bang hunter on head."

The axe was heavy. A single blow would split someone's skull. The thought made my stomach churn. And brought me back to my senses.

"Get back in the truck, Olki," I whispered, "and hold on tight."

I'd remembered something my karate teacher used to tell us before competitions. *The cunning snake beats the angry tiger.*

I would be the cunning snake.

Heart beating like a drum, I peered around the side of the Land Rover. The driver's door hung wide-open, and one of the Africans stood just on the other side of it, leaning against the front mudguard. Hooked over his shoulder was a short-barreled automatic rifle. It looked like an AK-47. I should have realized the poachers would have more than one firearm. The odds were really stacked against me. But I was the cunning snake. Surprise was on my side.

They thought I was lying unconscious in the back of the Land Rover.

I crept towards the unsuspecting poacher, keeping low so the door was between us. The axe felt sweaty in my hand. They'd left the engine running – probably to power the spotlight – so the man with the AK-47 didn't hear me when I slid into the driver's seat barely three feet from where he was standing. Keeping my head down, I checked out the gear lever, the pedals and the handbrake. Everything was much the same as my brother Nathan's Toyota, which I'd driven heaps of times.

I laid the axe on the seat beside me and inched my head up until I could see over the steering wheel. The second African stood on the other side of the Land Rover, just in front of the passenger door. It was open, too. Ideally, I'd have liked to shut both doors and lock them, but that would have given the game away. Anyway, there wasn't time. The white man had walked twenty yards up the trail to get a clear shot at the mother elephant, which had moved partially out of sight behind the mahogany tree.

I saw him raise the elephant gun to his shoulder and take aim.

Get a move on, Sam. Left foot on the clutch, right foot on the accelerator, slowly release the handbrake and …

Go, go, go!

With a clunk of gears and a mighty roar, the Land Rover leapt forward. Both doors slammed closed under the acceleration, but not before the one on my side smacked into the poacher with the AK-47, sending him flying. The other man dived in the opposite direction. I didn't see whether or not he got clear because I was looking straight ahead. The white man had spun around as soon as I hit the accelerator. He must have seen what had happened to his two friends. Eyes screwed up against the combined glare of the spotlight and the two headlights hurtling towards him out of the darkness, he pointed the elephant gun straight at me. There wasn't time to duck.

Boom!

The windshield exploded in a white spray of glass. It fell all over me like hailstones. But apart from a cut lip and a few small nicks to my bare chest and shoulders, I was unhurt. The bullet missed me by a couple of inches. I felt it whoosh past my left ear and crash through the window behind me. I hoped Olki was all right, but there wasn't time to check. The poacher stood in the middle of the trail, directly in my path, sliding another bullet into the breech of his rifle.

I hunched low in the driver's seat and stepped on the gas.

As the blinding lights rushed towards him, the expression on the poacher's face went through a range of emotions – first anger, then uncertainty, and finally blind panic. He turned and ran.

I chased him. I had no choice. He'd shoot me if I gave him half a chance. My foot was flat to the floor. Even in first gear, the roaring Land Rover was rapidly closing the distance. Ten yards, seven yards, five. If he was smart, the poacher would have swerved into the forest where the Land Rover couldn't follow, but he ran straight up the middle of the trail like a frightened rabbit, looking back over his shoulder as I came charging after him.

He should have been looking the other way.

"Look out!" I yelled, through the gaping hole where the Land Rover's windshield used to be, and slammed on the brakes.

My warning came too late. The poacher ran slap-bang into the baby elephant.

Its mother was standing right over it.

Before the startled ivory hunter knew what was happening, the mother elephant coiled her trunk around him and lifted him high in the air. He screamed and kicked his legs. His face was a mask of terror in the spotlight's beam as the elephant shook him like a rag doll. The rifle slipped from his hand and fell. It landed on the Land Rover's hood with a loud clunk. The elephant shook him a couple more times, then flung his limp body into the bushes on the other side of the trail.

I couldn't see the poacher from the Land Rover, but I knew he must be badly hurt. And he'd be dead in a matter of seconds if I didn't do something. The elephant was moving towards the bushes, no doubt to finish him off. Spinning the steering wheel to its full, right-hand lock, I accelerated directly across the elephant's path and slammed on the brakes, creating a road block. Now she couldn't get to her victim. Trumpeting in fury, she attacked the Land Rover instead.

Wham!

Four tons of elephant hit the passenger door head-on. The side of the vehicle rose off the ground.

I held onto the steering wheel and gritted my teeth. The elephant's big, wrinkly-edged eye looked in at me through the open window. I was sure she was going to tip us over. But she just rocked the Land Rover up and down a few times, then dropped it back onto its wheels with a mighty thump that sent the rifle skidding across the hood in front of me.

The elephant and I must have both noticed the rifle at the same moment. And both of us had the same idea. I climbed half-out of my seat and made a grab for it. But as my hand closed around the rifle's barrel, the elephant's big, leathery trunk encircled the wooden stock and wrenched the weapon from my grasp.

I don't know how intelligent elephants are, but she obviously knew what rifles did. They killed elephants. Swinging it in a big arc, she whacked the hateful thing against a tree. The stock shattered in a spaghetti of flying wood splinters, and the barrel bent into a u-shape. But the elephant still wasn't satisfied. She gathered the shattered weapon in her trunk and slammed it onto the ground. Then she knelt down and began grinding it into the dust with her head and her tusks and her trunk, all the time bellowing and trumpeting in rage.

I sat watching her for a few moments, feeling a mixture of awe (at her power), relief (that she hadn't killed me) and fear (that she still might). Then I snapped out of it. The elephant was around the other side of the Land Rover, totally distracted by her demolition job of the rifle. This was my chance to rescue the poacher and get out of there. I quietly opened the driver's door and slid out. The poacher lay in the bushes beside the trail, groaning and clutching his side. I took two steps towards him, tripped and fell headlong to the ground.

I was back on my feet in a moment. But not before I saw what had tripped me. A wire ran along the ground parallel to the edge of the trail. One end was tied around the trunk of a big, shadowy tree, the other end disappeared behind the Land Rover. It was too dark to see what was back there, but I could hear a snuffling noise, interspersed with small squeals. I realized that when I'd driven the Land Rover between the mother elephant and the poacher, I'd separated her from her calf as well.

The baby elephant's pitiful squeals reminded me why I'd come to Africa. Stepping over the wire,

I reached into the Land Rover for the axe. Then I raced over to the tree and chopped the wire. Or tried to. The axe was blunt – it bent the wire, but didn't cut it. I hit it again, harder this time. *Thwack!* It still didn't break. *Thwack! Thwack! Thwack!* I was getting desperate now. Instead of cutting the wire, the axe was burying it deeper and deeper into the soft bark of the mahogany tree. *Thwack! Thwack!*

Something touched me on the back. It was warm and wet and soft. I froze, the axe poised for another chop, and peered over my shoulder.

Shishkebab!

The calf was right behind me, gently exploring me with its trunk. But that wasn't what caused me to draw in my breath. Behind the calf, looming over both of us like a mountain, stood its mother.

MZUNGU!

None of us moved. I darted my eyes sideways, gauging whether or not I could make it back to the Land Rover. It was impossible. The mother elephant had me cold. She was standing right over me. I knew how fast she could move. All she had to do was reach out her trunk.

But she didn't. We were standing in semi-darkness – the Land Rover's lights were directed away from us – so I couldn't see her eyes. All I could see with my own, not-very-focused eye was her massive silhouette. Her calf touched me again with its trunk. *Please don't do that,* I thought nervously, knowing how protective its mother was. But the adult elephant did nothing except make a soft, rumbling noise. It didn't sound threatening.

Was it possible that she knew I was trying to free her calf?

Slowly, I turned back to the tree. If my hunch was right, she would let me cut the wire. If not … well, I was going to die.

Thwack! Thwack! Thwack! Thwack!

It took about ten more chops before – finally! – the wire snapped. I dropped the axe and pulled the wire clear of the tree. Now the calf was free to go. But it stayed where it was. And the mother stayed where she was, too.

"You're free," I said, backing slowly away in the direction of the Land Rover. "You can go."

The mother rumbled again, louder this time. She found the wire in the gloom and lifted it in her trunk. One end dangled free, but the other end was still attached to her calf's leg. She pulled on the wire, and the calf gave a squeal of pain.

I stopped. The mother wasn't going to come after me. She seemed to know I had tried to help her calf. I was free to climb into the Land Rover and drive away. But I couldn't just leave the baby elephant in the snare.

Slowly, I inched back towards the elephants. My heart was thumping in my chest. "Easy now," I said, as I came up to the calf. I lightly patted its head, then ran my hand along its bristly flank as I moved slowly around behind it. All the time I was speaking softly, saying stuff like, "Easy now, take it easy, I'm not going to hurt you," and hoping my tone of voice would let them know I was their friend. When I accidentally brushed against the mother's trunk with my shoulder, I thought I was cactus. But all she did was make another low, rumbly sound and take a step backwards.

I crouched next to the calf, running my hand lightly down its leg until I came to the wire. It was dark, and my eyesight was getting worse, so I had to feel rather than see. The wire noose was very tight and seemed to be embedded in the calf's skin. Below the wire, the calf's foot was sticky with blood. Working slowly, because I knew it must hurt, I found the wire slipknot and tried to loosen it. The calf squealed and behind me its mother rumbled in warning.

"Sorry," I said, half-expecting to be pulverized, but nothing happened.

Turning towards the mother, I found the loose end of the wire and pulled it towards me to get some slack. Then I gripped the slipknot again and tried feeding the wire back through it to free the noose from the calf's leg. But the knot was too tight – I couldn't budge it. The calf squealed again, and this time the mother's trunk came snuffling down across my shoulder to check out what I was doing to her baby. I froze, speaking softly to reassure her, as she ran her wet-tipped trunk all over me. It gave me an idea. I found the end of her trunk and wiped my hand across it a couple of times, making my palm wet and slimy. Then I rubbed the slime onto the wire where it fed into the slipknot. It acted as lubrication. When I pushed the wire again, I felt it start to slide through the knot. Suddenly, the noose fell to the ground, and the little elephant stepped free.

I waited beside the Land Rover while the mother herded the calf ahead of her up the trail. The calf wasn't limping, so the injury to its foot can't have been too bad. Just before she moved out of the spotlight's beam, the mother turned, raised her trunk high above her head and trumpeted. I reckon she was saying thank you. Then, silent as a ghost, she wheeled around and melted into the darkness. A frayed piece of fabric, the last remnant of my *Youth for Wildlife* shirt, fluttered to the ground where she'd stood.

I hurried to check on the injured poacher. He was barely conscious.

"Where's … elephant?" he breathed, his eyes swiveling nervously in their sockets.

"Don't worry, it's gone," I assured him.

He muttered something else that I didn't understand. He was obviously in a lot of pain.

"Try not to talk," I said. "I'll see where your mates are, then we'll lift you into the Land Rover."

But I didn't have to go looking for his friends. They came looking for me. I heard them before I saw them.

"Mzungu!"

I straightened and turned around. The two Africans stood in the shadows near the back of the Land Rover. One of them clutched his right elbow as if his arm was broken. The other held the AK-47.

Its evil black muzzle was pointed straight at me.

TRIGGER

Clangggg!

The man with the AK-47 didn't see what hit him. For a moment he stood motionless, holding the rifle in a dramatic pose like a statue on a war memorial, then he collapsed in a heap.

Olki jumped out of the rear of the Land Rover with the folding shovel in one hand. He raised it threateningly at the second African and spoke rapidly in Swahili. The frightened poacher shook his head, mumbled a few words in reply, then sat on the ground next to his fallen comrade.

Olki picked up the AK-47 and brought it over to me. "Hunters no more trouble," he said.

It took several minutes to get everyone into the Land Rover. The second African had a broken collarbone, so Olki and I had to do all the lifting. The man Olki had KO'd with the shovel was still unconscious, and the white man was so knocked around that he could barely move. We laid both of them in the back among the elephant tusks, then we cleared out all the tools from the tool box in case the African woke up and got any bright ideas. I made the other African ride in the front with us, where we could keep an eye on him. His shoulder must have been very painful, but I wasn't taking any chances – I told Olki, who was sitting in the middle, to keep his shovel ready. And I jammed the AK-47 between the driver's seat and the door, where only I could reach it.

"Next stop, police station," I said confidently, and put the Land Rover into gear.

My plan was to deliver the poachers and the elephant tusks to the police at the first town we came to, then go looking for a hospital or a doctor. But my eyesight was getting very bad. I could hardly see twenty yards ahead. I stopped the Land Rover.

"Olki, can you drive?"

"Drive truck?" He sounded incredulous.

Silly me. Of course he couldn't drive. He came from a tiny village half a day's walk from the nearest road. And he was only ten years old. Even I couldn't drive when I was ten.

"Do you think you can steer?" I asked.

Olki became my eyes. He sat on my lap and steered, while I operated the gears and pedals. It seemed to work. For about thirty uneventful seconds, we bounced down the bumpy trail, picking up speed and gathering confidence every foot of the way. I had just changed up to second gear when Olki and the African in the seat beside us simultaneously yelled out:

"Chui!"

The Land Rover swerved sharply as Olki spun the steering wheel, and I instinctively slammed on the brakes. We slewed to a halt in the middle of the trail, almost at right angles to the direction we'd been traveling. It was a miracle we hadn't rolled. *Chui.* My brain didn't need to translate from Swahili – the man-eater was so close that I could see it, even though the headlights were shining away from it into the forest. It was standing just below my window, its horrible, scarred face looking up at me. Olki must have swerved to *miss* it! It was the worst thing he could have done. Now we were stationary, and all the windows, including the windshield, were wide-open. Meals on wheels. Maybe not. I reached for the AK-47 and tugged. But it was wedged between my seat and the door and wouldn't budge. In desperation, I tried the window winder knob, but the rifle's big, crescent-shaped magazine was jammed against it.

The man-eater growled. Its tail twitched.

Olki slid off my lap and offered me the shovel. I shook my head. A shovel might be effective against poachers, but it was no match for a man-eating leopard. I had another idea. It was our only hope. I still had my foot on the clutch, so the Land Rover's engine was still running. Shifting my other foot from the brake to the accelerator, I stamped it all the way to the floor and spun the steering wheel. Engine roaring, the Land Rover lurched in a semicircle, narrowly missing the trees at the edge of the trail. But I'd forgotten it was in second gear, and we didn't accelerate fast enough. A large, spotted shape flashed past my window and landed – *thump* – on the front of the Land Rover. The African yelped in terror, and Olki raised the shovel. We were hurtling down the trail with the man-eater on the hood. Belly flat against the metal and paws spread wide for balance, it came scrabbling towards us. There was no windshield. We were sitting ducks!

I stamped on the brakes. The Land Rover skidded to a halt. But the leopard kept going. It went sliding away from us, its claws squealing on the paintwork, then it toppled over the front of the hood and disappeared. But it was only gone for a moment. With a roar that rattled my eardrums, the man-eater leapt back onto the Land Rover.

The engine had stalled. Nothing was going to stop it this time.

I flung my door open and rolled out, yelling to attract the leopard's attention.

Time slowed right down. My whole life flashed before my eyes as I lost my footing and landed flat on my back in a crunchy bed of leaves and grass. Winded, I lay looking up at a sky full of fuzzy white stars.

Where was the man-eater?

"*Saaaaaaaaaam!*" Olki cried out, in a strange, slowed-down voice that seemed to echo across the universe. "*Saaaaaaaam, looooook ouuuuuuut!*"

The stars disappeared. The sky seemed to fall on top of me, and everything went black.

I pulled the trigger.

A WORLD WITHOUT ANIMALS

REIGN OF TERROR ENDS

A young wildlife ambassador has ended the reign of terror that has gripped a large part of Western Tanzania for the past eighteen months.

Samuel Fox (14), from Australia, fatally shot the Chui Hills man-eating leopard on Tuesday evening. The rogue leopard was responsible for the deaths of five people.

Mr. Fox was traveling to the International Youth for Wildlife Conference in Marusha when he became separated from his bus. Aided by local resident, Olkilia Nyambui (10), Mr. Fox used a firearm confiscated from illegal ivory hunters to rid Tanzania of the most notorious man-eater in living memory. The three poachers are being held in police custody in Marusha.

Police spokesman, Sergeant Francis Iboti, commended the two young men for their bravery.

Mr. Fox, who spent last night in Marusha Hospital receiving treatment for temporary blindness following an encounter with a deadly spitting cobra, said he regretted killing the leopard.

"Leopards are beautiful animals," he said. "But it would have killed me and my companions, so I had no choice."

Today, he and Mr. Nyambui will be special guests at the International Youth for Wildlife Conference, where Mr. Fox will be speaking about efforts in his country to save the endangered Australian bilby.

Mr. Fox believes that young people worldwide should become involved in wildlife conservation.

"A world without wild animals would be a pretty boring place," he said.

ABOUT THE AUTHOR

Born in New Zealand, Justin D'Ath is one of twelve children. He came to Australia in 1971 to study for the missionary priesthood. After three years, he left the seminary in the dead of night and spent two years roaming Australia on a motorcycle. While doing that he began writing for motorcycle magazines. He published his first novel for adults in 1989. This was followed by numerous award-winning short stories, also for adults. Justin has worked in a sugar mill, on a cattle station, in a mine, on an island, in a laboratory, built cars, picked fruit, driven forklifts and taught writing for twelve years. He wrote his first children's book in 1996. To date he has published twenty-four books. He has two children, two grandchildren, and one dog.

www.justindath.com

Private Investigator
Book #3

MESS AT LOCH NESS
by Dwayne J. Ferguson

Just Us Books, Inc.
East Orange, New Jersey
www.justusbooks.com

Printed in Canada
12 11 10 9 8 7 6 5
Library of Congress Cataloging-in-Publication
data is available.

ISBN: 0-940975-74-2 (paperback)

He's smart!
He's cool!
He's a detective!
And he's a kid!

Kid Caramel's on the case again. But this time, his mystery is international. His friend's grandfather is missing, and Kid and his best friend Earnie offer to lead the search for him—thousands of miles away in Scotland!

Kid Caramel is out of his element in this unfamiliar land of castles and lords. Then there are the strange noises in his friend's castle; the suspicious behavior of family friends; and of course tales of the infamous Loch Ness monster.

Who, or what, is responsible for Grandpa's disappearance? Kid is facing the ultimate case. Will his sleuthing skills be enough to solve this trans-Atlantic mystery?

Chapter One:
For Whom the Bell Tolls

Caramel Parks counted down the seconds on the large round wall clock. Ten-nine-eight…a few more seconds and the boy detective and his companions would be free!

FREE!

Seven-six-five…they weren't going to get any more answers out of him or his friends for a long time. No power on Earth could stop what was going to happen in five measly seconds… four-three-two-one….

RRRRIIIIIIIIIIIIIIIIIIIIIIIIIIIINNNNNNNNNN GGGGGGGGGGG!!!!!!!!

"Summer vacation at last!" yelled Caramel. He grabbed his book bag from the floor and swung it over his shoulder. His book bag accidentally slammed into the arm of Earnie Todd,

Caramel's best friend on the planet. Earnie, in turn, jumped a foot backward and crashed into Kayin McIntyre. Kayin's books rained down to the classroom floor and all three boys laughed at the chain reaction.

Kayin McIntyre was an exchange student from Scotland. On Kayin's very first day in his new school, Sharktooth Williams, the resident bully, insulted his Scottish accent. Kayin immediately hurled an insult back at Sharktooth, leaving the bully in total, drooling shock. Caramel and Earnie had known right away that the three of them, Earnie, Caramel and Kayin, would become the best of friends in no time flat.

"Hey, watch it, Kid. That's my pen arm," said Earnie, rubbing his right shoulder. Earnie carefully pushed a black pen, trimmed in gold (a birthday gift from his parents), back down into his shirt pocket.

"How am I supposed to be the school paper's star reporter if my arm's all busted up?"

"I think you'll live," Caramel said sarcastically. He backed away just in time to miss a

6

mini-stampede of students on their way out of the school.

"Hey, Kayin, it seemed like vacation would never get here, huh?" Earnie asked.

"Yeah, it was like the hands on the clock were moving in sloooowwww moootion, like the Matrix," Kayin said. The trio laughed.

"Well, I'm going to start my vacation off by going to the dentist," said Earnie with a great big smile. Caramel and Kayin suddenly stopped laughing and stared at Earnie as if he'd grown another eye in the middle of his head.

Caramel's eyebrow arched in surprise. "That's an, uh, weird way to start a vacation. And you look a little too happy about going to the dentist," said Caramel.

"That's because if he doesn't find any cavities, he gives you toy cars," replied Earnie. Kayin and Caramel exchanged glances and both turned again to Earnie, who had lost his mind.

"That's nice…and if the dentist does find cavities, you'll wish you were in a real car, going as fast as you can in the opposite direction," said Caramel, laughing.

Kayin was about to add his own jokes about his weird American friend when his cell phone rang. Kayin smiled and unclipped the phone from his belt.

Kayin whispered to his friends that it was his dad on the phone. Kayin and his father exchanged a few words before tears formed in Kayin's eyes. He slowly put the phone away and turned to his friends.

"I've got to go home right now," he said, wiping his eyes. He simply stared at the floor.

Caramel and Earnie moved closer. "Bro, what's the matter?" asked Caramel.

Kayin sighed and said softly, "My grandfather is missing...and I have to go home."

Caramel placed his hand on Kayin's shoulder in support of his friend. "We'll go with you if you want, right, Earn'?" Earnie nodded, feeling a little sad himself.

"Thanks, guys," Kayin started, "but I mean I have to go all the way home...to Scotland."

Meanwhile...

Across the ocean, in the highlands of Scotland, a dark shape stood in the window of McIntyre Castle. Through high-power binocu-

8

lars, the shadow watched the dark distant water of Loch Ness, which was several miles away, churn like boiling oil. The shape looked something like a man, but not quite. It stood eight feet tall and floated above the floor like a black cloud of doom. The shape turned to look down at his latest victim and laughed. He focused his attention once more on the lake.

"Soon, my pet…soon, you shall be mine!" The shape tilted his head back and laughed hard enough to fill the air for miles around. **"BWAhahahahahahahahahahahahahahahah!"**

Chapter Two:
Four Guys and an Ocean

"Flight 749 to Glasgow, Scotland, now boarding at Gate 7B," a voice said over the intercom.

Caramel loved the airport. He always pretended that it was a space station in orbit high above the Earth. Caramel was, of course, the captain of the space station.

"Well, boys, that's us," said Mr. Ronald Parks, Caramel's father. He folded his newspaper under his arm and rounded up the gang, their tickets, and their luggage. Mr. Parks held all of their passports and let the boys board the plane before he did to keep his eyes on them. The last thing he needed was to hire a detective to find his detective son and his friends in a foreign country.

The Parks family had gone on a trip to Egypt three summers earlier and it was the first time they had ever received passports. Of course, Caramel, being the detective, started searching the Internet for as many unsolved worldwide mysteries as he could.

They all found their assigned seats on the jumbo jet and buckled up. The plane was so huge, Caramel wondered how it would ever get off the ground. It looked like the wings stretched from the passenger cabin to halfway around the world.

"The best part of flying is takeoff!" Caramel said. The boys had come up with a round-trip seating plan: Caramel would sit in the window seat on the way to Scotland. Kayin would have the window seat on the flight back to America. Earnie wanted the aisle seat and to be as far away from the window as he could get. Far away...as in back in the airport watching the plane take off without him on it.

A chime sounded a soft 'diiiing doonnngg' to get the attention of all the passengers aboard the plane. The captain had a voice like a TV wrestling commentator. "L-l-ladies and gentle-men, this-s-s is your captain-n-n. We are cleared for takeoff-f-f. Plea-s-se fasten all safety belts. En-n-njoy your fliiight."

11

'Diiiiing donnng.'

The engines roared and all of the passengers were pushed gently back in their seats as the plane raced down the runway, at what felt to Caramel like two billion miles per hour. The runway turned into a gray and yellow blur and then they were off the ground.

"Warp engines engage!" yelled Caramel.

"Keep it down, son," said Mr. Parks. He unfolded his newspaper and started reading. Earnie was looking straight ahead. He wasn't even blinking.

"Hey, Kayin, do you recognize this statue?" Caramel said, pointing to Earnie. Caramel was trying to make the trip home less stressful for Kayin, although he knew it would be hard to do.

"What's the matter, afraid of flying, Earnie?" asked Kayin.

Earnie barely managed a nod.

"Here, try reading something," said Mr. Parks. He handed Earnie the comics section from his newspaper. "It helps to take your mind off being up here."

Earnie's hand slowly reached for the paper

as if he was moving through syrup.

"Hey, cool! We're already over the ocean," said Caramel. "It's huuuuge! Look, Earn...I think I see Godzilla doing the backstroke down there." Earnie didn't budge.

Earnie couldn't care less if Godzilla was playing NFL football outside the window.

"I bet you can get a great story for the school paper about your trip across the Atlantic Ocean," said Kayin.

"Kayin's right, you know. Who else will have a scoop like this when we go back to school in September? You could call it Trans- Atlantic Battle Against Ghosts!" said Caramel.

Then a spark, a hint of life crackled in Earnie's brain. Earnie managed a blink, and then it looked as if he was starting to breathe again. Before anyone knew it, Earnie had whipped out his notebook and pen.

"You guys are right! I'll be the man this year...yeah, the MAN!" Then Earnie, the reporter, was scribbling notes as he leaned over Mr. Parks, Kayin, and Caramel to look out of the window. "Out of my way, I have great journalism to craft here!"

Shortly after Earnie came back to the land of the living, a flight attendant strolled down the aisle passing out headphones. A second attendant followed offering half-cups of soda (actually two drops of soda under a glacier of ice, thought Caramel) and teeny bags of peanuts.

"I don't know about you guys, but I'm getting some headphones," said Caramel. "The entertainment schedule says that the Falcon Shadow show is coming on in ten minutes, so leave all messages with my secretary." Although Caramel had the headphones on, he stared out the window at the clouds.

Caramel took out his notepad. The young detective read over the notes he had written since Kayin's grandfather vanished.

Kid Caramel: Private Investigator
Case File: Kayin's Missing Grandfather

I never would have thought that one of my best friends would wind up becoming a client. But Kayin's grandfather is suddenly missing. There's no way I'm going to stand by when I can use my skills as a detective to help!

Kayin showed me some pictures of his grandfather, a man by the name of Ewan McIntyre, late seventies. Mr. McIntyre seemed like a regular kind of guy so I freaked out when Kayin told me that his grandfather may have been grabbed by ghosts! It seems that Kayin's grandfather was installing a new display of medieval books when he suddenly vanished. All that was left behind was the medallion of the family emblem.

I immediately asked my parents if we could go to help Kayin. I knew the hard part would be convincing them to let us go to another country by ourselves but my father had a plan. He took a week off from his entertainment law firm so he could take us himself. He said that Earnie and I were great friends to go all out to help a buddy so he set the whole trip up.

Mom packed us some lunch...I may be a good detective, but I still can't figure out what kind of sandwiches these are.

End case file for now.

After six hours and several episodes with air turbulence, the plane was preparing to land. Caramel started reflecting about how he had solved all of his past mysteries. He went over all the steps for finding clues. He remembered all of the little mistakes bad guys always seemed to make. But now he had a new enemy to face and a new mystery to solve in a land he didn't know. Now Kid Caramel, private investigator, wondered what ghosts looked like. And how he would catch one.

Chapter Three:
The International Scareport

As the plane prepared for landing, Caramel switched to "Foreign Language Translation Mode." When Kayin had first arrived in America as a foreign exchange student, it had been very difficult for Caramel to understand much of what Kayin said. Kayin told Caramel that if he thought his Scottish accent was thick, he should hear the older folks talk. Kayin's accent was much less difficult to understand because he watched a lot of American movies and television. His parents, on the other hand, rarely left their small farm and found such entertainment unnecessary.

Everything Caramel could see out the window was green for miles. Tiny houses spotted the countryside. There were tiny sheep grazing along the Highlands and lots of rolling fog hugging miniature mountains. Every once in a while, he could see a lake, known as a loch in Scotland, populated by tiny fishing boats.

The plane touched down at Inverness Airport with a small bump. After a short taxi down the runway, the plane pulled up to the gate and the seatbelt signal finally blinked off.

Caramel shook the Captain's hand as he left the plane. "Flawless piloting through the Alpha Quadrant, lieutenant," Caramel said in his starship captain's voice. "We barely escaped the Borg, but thanks to your skills, we made it. I'll talk to my connections at StarFleet and put you in for a promotion."

The captain smiled and tapped Caramel on the back. "I'll be sure to keep the Enterprise warmed up for you, Captain," the plane's real captain said.

As the group made their way to the gate, Kayin's eyes moved rapidly around the airport as he tried to spot his father. There were dozens of people waiting for their friends and loved ones at the gate. One gentleman was nearly seven feet tall and had a beard and head of hair as red as Kayin's. "There he is, guys!" Kayin

18

said as a familiar face smiled and waved at them.

"Ahh, welcome home, Kayin, m'boy!" said Mr. McIntyre. The muscular giant of a man picked his son off the ground as if he weighed no more than half an ounce. He wrapped his son in a huge bear hug that engulfed his entire body.

Kayin blushed and smiled, embarrassed at being hugged in the airport. "Uh, hi Dad. These are my friends: Caramel Parks, Mr. Ronald Parks, and Earnie Todd. Everybody, this is my father, Wallace McIntyre." Mr. Parks had to look up, almost to the ceiling, to look Mr. McIntyre in the eye as he shook the tall man's hand.

"Any word on Grandfather?" Kayin asked his father. Kayin was still a mile up in the air until his father finally put him down.

"Not yet, son, but the police are on the case. We have posters with your grandfather's picture on it all over town. Hopefully someone will ring us soon." Mr. McIntyre pointed to the public phone section of the airport. He had placed one of the posters there the moment he walked into the terminal. There was a picture of Grandpa McIntyre standing next to two people in the poster. Behind them was an ancient castle.

"Who are the other people in the poster, Mr. McIntyre?" asked Caramel, who was now officially on duty as a detective. His brain camera took a snapshot of them. Then he remembered the real digital camera his father owned. Caramel asked to use it, then took a snapshot of the poster.

"Oh, this picture was taken at the family picnic last month. Those are our good friends, the Cragmires. The missus is our business attorney," said Mr. McIntyre. "You see, we own the McIntyre Castle, a very popular tourist attraction. The entire family pitches in to operate it." Caramel's detective intuition tingled.

Something wasn't quite right about that poster…there were tiny greenish smudges in both corners where the poster was fastened to the wall with strips of tape. To help him think, he popped his familiar sugar-free banana bubblegum in his mouth.

"I sure hope he's OK. I miss him," said Kayin in a whisper.

"Shall we grab our luggage and then start for home?" asked Mr. McIntyre. The group

picked up their belongings from the airport terminal carousels and then headed to the parking
lot.

Kayin's father owned a blue minivan,
which looked like it had plenty of room for the
whole bunch of them, plus a few more. The sun
was starting to set and more fog hovered over
the airport grounds.

The first thing Caramel noticed as they
exited the airport was the cool Scottish air. It
was June, and in the USA it was about eighty
degrees on average. In Scotland, it was around
sixty degrees, but that was only the temperature
for that one day. Scottish weather was extremely
unpredictable, so tomorrow it could rain, hail,
snow, or be hot enough for swimming. Caramel
was glad they had all packed light sweaters,
shorts, and even boots (although they were
hoping Kayin had been making up the part
about the snow).

The group approached the minivan and
Caramel noticed a note under one of the windshield wiper blades. Caramel didn't want to
appear rude so he waited for Mr. McIntyre to
retrieve the note.

Mr. McIntyre unfolded the green sheet of

21

paper. His mouth dropped open.

"What does it say, sir?" asked Kid Caramel, his anticipation building.

"The note says to get in the car and play the tape that's in the deck."

A lot of worried glances passed back and forth within the small group.

"Well, if this has to do with your grandfather, we'd best listen to the tape," said Mr. McIntyre. He pulled out the car keys and carefully opened the door. He checked the car out before allowing the rest of the group to get in.

Mr. McIntyre sighed and pressed the play button on the tape deck. There was silence and then suddenly the tape sprang to life at top volume…

"Be waaaaaaaaaaarrrrnnned…McIntyre Cassssstle belongs to usss nowwwww…It is forevvvverrr currsssed and haaaauuuunnnnted…," said a voice that sounded like it was colder than ice. "Ssstay thee awaaayyy…or endure ourrr wraaaaathhhhh!!!!" Then the tape went silent after a small hiss.

"What in the world was that?" asked Kayin's father.

"I don't know," said Mr. Parks. "I've never heard anything like it before…and I hope I never do again."

"Aye, indeed," agreed Mr. McIntyre.

"Do you see what I see, guys?" asked Caramel.

There was a slimy green goo under the windshield wiper blade. Before anyone could blink, Earnie exited the car and scooped the slime up with a plastic spoon. He then placed the spoon in a plastic bag. Kid Caramel was outside in a flash. Kayin soon joined them both.

"Oh, yeah, Kayin did mention that your son was something of a sleuth," said Mr. McIntyre to Mr. Parks.

"Yup, even the local police in our town know about his hobby. They even call him Kid Caramel."

After collecting the clue, the boys climbed back into the car.

Kid Caramel examined the green goo. It was thick and slimy and left a trail as it slid down the plastic bag. "This might be ectoplasm, the stuff left behind by ghosts," said Kid Caramel, smiling. Only he would find something cool in that discovery.

"This isn't good...not good at all," said Earnie. He checked his hands to make sure he hadn't gotten ectoplasm on them when he collected the sample.

"Could we go to the castle? I'd like to look around," said Caramel.

"I'm sure I can arrange that," said Mr. McIntyre with a slight smile. He was trying to be brave, but deep inside he missed his father terribly. "We'll go by there, but not till morning. "I don't want to make any more spirits angry with us. They come out at night, y'see... and the night belongs to them, aye!"

Those words sent a chill down everybody's spines, including Caramel's. Nobody said a word during the trip along the A96 highway. There were empty seats in the minivan and nobody wanted to invite spirits to fill them up.

Mr. McIntyre drove down the scenic road until they reached the city called Inverness. The town shared the same name as the airport, though they were miles apart from each other. Kayin explained that the word Inverness meant 'mouth of Ness,' because it sat at the tip of Loch Ness.

24

According to the legend of Loch Ness, the lake is occupied by a monster. The Loch Ness Monster, or "Nessie" for short, has been allegedly sighted by people for hundreds of years. But no one has ever had any concrete proof of the monster's existence.

Before the trip, Caramel read every book he could find about Nessie in the school's library. From countless eyewitness reports, the monster supposedly looks like a prehistoric dinosaur known as a pleisiosaur. It is said to have a long neck like a giraffe, a body like a seal, and four flippers used for swimming. The monster has been reported to be about the size of a school bus. People claim the monster has even eaten live sheep!

Trees hung menacingly over the roads they traveled, and every once in a while, you could hear something splashing in the loch. Kid Caramel wondered if those splashes could be the famous Loch Ness Monster. Every once in a while, they would drive past a billboard inviting tourists to try searching for Nessie.

The sky suddenly became very dark as the group entered Loch end. Far through the trees and down a hill, they could see Loch

Ness. Another chill went down Earnie's spine. Caramel was silent, looking everywhere for the Loch Ness Monster. But, that would have to wait.

Tomorrow he had a date with ghosts in an ancient and cold castle.

The McIntyres lived in a small farmhouse a few miles east of Inverness. Their Highlands home was surrounded by a homemade wooden fence. Lush grass, tall hedges, and cherry blossom trees surrounded either side of the house. Caramel noted that almost every house in Loch end was tiny and looked like something out of a fantasy novel. They reminded him of houses he had read about in *The Hobbit.*

In the distance he saw sheep and a few horses wandering about. As everyone piled out of the van, two dogs, both collies, raced up to greet them.

"C'mere boys, c'mon!" Kayin said, slapping his legs and whistling to the dogs. He grabbed the dogs and rolled on the ground with them. "These are my dogs, Fireball and Chase, guys."

Caramel and Earnie petted the dogs and

soon all the boys were rolling along the ground in a big ball of kids, grass, and fur.

A short and slightly plump woman opened the front door. She looked at the pile of kids on the grass, but her eyes locked onto the one with the fire-red hair.

"How about a big hug for your mom, laddie," she said as Kayin ran into her open arms.

"I missed you, Mom," Kayin said. Nothing felt as good as a mother's hug. "This is my mom, Molly McIntyre, everybody. Mom, this is Earnie, Caramel, and his dad, Mr. Ronald Parks."

"Nice to meet you all," she said with a warm smile. "Well, folks, make yourselves at home. Don't be shy and if you're thirsty or hungry, treat the fridge as your own," she added.

Earnie took her up on the offer and was already sorting through the contents of the fridge.

Out of the corner of his eye, Caramel spotted something in the fridge. "Is that a shepherd's pie?" he asked. Caramel loved the combo of beef and vegetables in a potato crust.

"Kayin told me you were readin' up on all things Scottish, lad," said Mrs. McIntyre with a smile. "Kayin told me how your mouth watered when ye read about our famous shepherd's pie."

"You made this for me?" Caramel asked, shoving Earnie out of the way.

"Heyyyy, I want some of that too!" said Earnie.

Caramel had no problem sharing the pie with anyone who wanted some.

"I hear that you boys are quite the detectives," said Mrs. McIntyre, making several sandwiches and a pitcher of fresh squeezed lemonade. She searched the refrigerator for ingredients to prepare a spinach and bacon quiche.

"Yes, ma'am. We have solved every mystery we've been on," said the kid detective. "That's why they call me Kid Caramel." In his mind, Caramel heard theme music play at the mention of his title.

"They thought I was the werewolf in the last case!" said Kayin, laughing up a storm.

"Uh, only Earnie thought that," said Caramel, pointing to his best friend.

"Heyyy!" shouted Earnie.

"Show the boys around the house, son,"

said Mr. McIntyre. He turned to Mr. Parks. "Ronald, how about a game of chess?"

Mr. Parks and Mr. McIntyre headed to the den while Mrs. McIntyre rounded up things to prepare dinner.

Caramel and Earnie followed Kayin as he pointed out old photos and mementos that hung on the walls and sat on curio cabinets. Caramel took mental snapshots of each item with his brain camera. The McIntyres' house was warm and comfortable with little knick-knacks in almost every corner. Every floor was covered with thick handmade rugs. The boys made their way upstairs.

"This is my grandfather's room," said Kayin, turning on the light. The room was the size of the others but cluttered with tons of junk. There were books and fishing equipment all over the place. There didn't seem to be a spot where clutter hadn't taken root. Earnie wondered how the basement wound up upstairs by mistake.

Caramel switched to "Scanning Mode" and swept the room several times. He was looking for any clues that would indicate that Grandpa McIntyre had been taken from the house by force. So far, he hadn't found evidence such as a broken window or doors. The mess in the room looked pretty much deliberate. It didn't look like stuff was tossed around in search of something.

Kayin was suddenly very quiet as he thought about how much he missed his grandfather. Caramel elbowed him in the side of his stomach.

"Don't worry, buddy, we'll get your grandfather back. Ghosts or no ghosts."

"I vote for the no ghosts option," added Earnie with a nervous smile.

About an hour later, Mrs. McIntyre announced that dinner was ready and would be tossed out the window if no one came to the table in five minutes. She didn't have to worry much, since the house was full of hungry men and boys. In less than one minute every seat had a person in it, which made Mrs. McIntyre smile. Even Kayin's dogs made an appearance and sat within range of whatever scraps might be heading their way.

The dinner table has enough food on it to feed the entire planet, thought Caramel. He looked out the window to see if a line of people with plates had started forming.

Mrs. McIntyre had cooked a little of everything, from Scottish to American food. The table was miles high with stovies (a potato, meat, and vegetables dish), quiche, hot dogs, and hamburgers. There was even some potato salad thrown in for good measure. Earnie ran away from the haggis, a pocket of sheep's lungs, heart, and liver boiled and sewn in a sheep's stomach.

For dessert they had black bun, a kind of fruit cake, and flummery. Caramel really liked the flummery, which was a dessert made of orange rinds, honey, oatmeal, and cream. He jotted down a note to ask his mom to make some for him when he returned home.

Mr. McIntyre patted his full stomach. "Now that was a meal fit for a small village, sweetie," he said to his wife, who was blushing.

"Thank you, kind sir," she said with a chuckle that brought rosiness to her cheeks.

"I agree, the meal was wonderful, Molly," said Mr. Parks. He pushed his chair away from the table to make room for his full stomach.

Mr. McIntyre looked at the wall clock.

31

"Well, you boys go off and get some shuteye. I'll keep an eye out for the spirits," said Mr. McIntyre with a smile. Mr. and Mrs. McIntyre rose and started collecting the dirty dishes. She smiled at the boys and waved as she headed off to the kitchen.

"Good night, guys," said Mr. Parks. He got up and gave each of the boys noogies on their heads.

"Good night," the boys said in reply. Mr. Parks walked to the kitchen to lend a hand.

Since the topic of the day had been spirits, and nasty ones, at that, the boys agreed that a tent in Kayin's room would be the base of operations. There the three could look after one another.

Kayin closed his room door after the boys piled in.

"I sure hope my grandfather is OK," Kayin said.

"Don't worry, we'll find him. I promise!" said Caramel.

"Yup, we'll find him and he'll be waiting for us!" added Earnie confidently.

"Well, I'll see you guys in the morning. I'll

try to dream up some strategies," said Caramel as he covered up in a thick wool blanket. The wool made him itch but he managed to ignore it.

The boys tossed and turned a little until, one by one, they drifted off to sleep. Everyone, that is, except Kid Caramel. His brain was preparing to go ghost hunting.

Chapter Four:
A Date with a Ghost

Early the next morning, Earnie, Kayin, Caramel, Mr. Parks, and Mr. McIntyre piled into the family van. Mr. McIntyre took highway A82, a road that hugged the 23-mile stretch of Loch Ness. Soon, they approached the famous Urquhart Castle, where many residents and tourists alike claim to have spotted "Nessie." They traveled a few miles more until finally reaching McIntyre Castle.

McIntyre Castle sat high atop a windy hill. Centuries ago, the height allowed defenders to see the enemy approaching from a distance. When the sun hit the castle a certain way, it looked like a shadowy set of dragon jaws against the sky. The road leading up to the drawbridge looked like a long tongue. To Caramel, it was one of the most amazing sights he had ever seen. He took his badge out of his backpack and pinned it to his jacket.

As usual, Caramel was prepared for

his case. Before leaving America, he had done extensive research on castles. He noticed that the castle was of the double-wall type, with a lower wall of battlements standing in front of a much higher wall. Built this way, two sets of medieval archers could rain arrows from long-bows and crossbows down on enemies.

A large ring of filled-in earth surrounded the grounds, probably a moat in its past life. Caramel wondered if the moat was the kind filled with water or sharp pointed spikes. Either option would have been bad news for invaders.

"Did your family actually live in the castle when it was constructed, Mr. McIntyre?" Caramel asked. He turned on the recorder inside his brain.

"Sure did, young man. They even participated in battles to defend the castle from invaders," said Mr. McIntyre. He drove the van up the winding path that lead to the castle entrance.

The main entrance, called a gatehouse, was where some of the castle's strongest defenses were kept. One was called the portcullis, a huge gate that could be closed in a hurry if enemy troops tried to rush inside. Behind this were heavy double doors which would trap attackers and position them right under specially positioned holes in the ceiling known as murder holes. From there, defenders could pour red hot sand, boiling water, stones, and even hot oil on the heads of their enemies.

Everyone piled out of the minivan. The ground was cold, even through the thick soles of his sneakers, observed Caramel. The guys headed up the manicured hedge path to the castle. The path was lined with copper beech and pine trees, as well as several varieties of multi-colored flowers.

Kid Caramel switched to "Bio-Scan Mode" and swept the castle grounds with his bionically enhanced eyesight. High above, gliding as if they had no care in the world, were red kites, relatives of the eagle. The large birds rarely flapped their wings, which were spotted with white patches.

The only sound came from the flapping of light blue flags atop the spires of the castle turrets. A golden 'M' for McIntyre was emblazoned in the center of each flag along with the seal of a wolf. Caramel smiled at the wolf, which reminded him of his last adventure. He thought that maybe, just maybe, there was more to the Kayin-as-a-werewolf thing than he thought.

A large loch swirled several hundred yards away. It wasn't Loch Ness, but it sure looked as moody. Kid Caramel ran another bio-scan of the loch area. Bingo! There was a group of people standing on the shore below. They were using all kinds of high-tech gadgetry: computers, speakers, and video cameras. There was a large sign that read 'Monster Watchers' posted in the mud next to their tent. Under the words, there was a picture of a dinosaur-like creature with a long neck and humps on its back.

Caramel took a mental snapshot of the scene with his brain camera. Ka-click!

Caramel's father and Mr. McIntyre walked over to speak with the police who had gathered at the scene. The police were investigating Grandpa McIntyre's disappearance. Mr. McIntyre and Mr. Parks wanted to talk to the authorities about the latest news in the case. There were several other officers looking for clues around the giant castle grounds. Some of the officers had German shepherds and others carried cameras. Every so often, a TV reporter was shooed away by the police.

Mr. Parks and Mr. McIntyre walked up to a few of the detectives. They were holding up a piece of torn cloth. One detective motioned for a uniformed officer to come over to him.

"Take this and send it to the lab downtown," said the senior detective. As the officer put the cloth in a plastic bag, another officer approached Mr. McIntyre.

"Good morning, Mr. McIntyre. Headquarters told me that you'd be here today. I have something to show you regarding this case," said Officer McHale. Kid Caramel's ears perked up at the announcement. The boys and their fathers gathered around the officer.

"Is it anything bad, officer? Is my father OK?" asked Mr. McIntyre, concerned and worried at the news.

"I don't think bad is the word…weird is, though. Please, this way," he said as the men followed.

"What's going on, Father?" asked Kayin.

"I don't know yet, Kayin," his father answered as the group followed the officer.

"Uh, we received this tape a few minutes ago in our squad car," answered Officer McHale. We don't know how it got in there but

38

it's got this weird green goo on it."

"Not again!" Caramel said. He took out his notepad.

Earnie slapped his own forehead. Kayin braced himself.

They arrived at the police car and Officer McHale pressed the play button on the tape deck.

The voice on the tape quivered, "Yoouuuuuu haaaave beeeeen waaaarrrrnnnned. Yoouuu musssssst sellllllll McIntyrrrrre Cassssstle innn one hourrrrrr.... orrr yoouuu willlll nevvvverrr sssseeeeee thhhhe McIntyrrrre granddddfatherrrrrr aliiiiivvvve againnnnnn. Weee expecttt toooo seeeee the cassstle forrrr saalllllle onnn the Interrrrnetttt in fffiiifty-ninnneee minutesssssss...."

"Oh, no, it's the ghost! What are you gonna do, Father?" asked Kayin nervously. He was biting his fingers.

Mr. McIntyre slowly shook his head. "Well, according to my attorneys, the castle hasn't been making any profit lately, and we're almost broke. And now, my father is missing. It looks like this castle is nothing but trouble. Ronald, you're an attorney, would you mind coming with me to meet the Cragmires?"

"No problem, my friend," replied Mr. Parks.

"The castle has been in our family for generations, but my father means more to me than this old stone building," said Mr. McIntyre. "I have no choice but to sell the castle."

"Officer McHale, would you mind keeping an eye on the boys for a little while?" asked Mr. Parks.

"You got it, sir," said the policeman. McHale gathered his unit and gave them orders to question tourists in the area. Now he could focus all of his attention on watching the kids.

Mr. Parks and Mr. McIntyre got in the minivan and headed for the business district of Inverness.

"Well, fellas, how about a tour of the castle? You can tag along with us and help look for clues," said Officer McHale.

Kid Caramel was about to reply when suddenly something caught his attention.

"Everybody, look up there!" he said, pointing to a window in the castle wall.

"Woah! What is that thing?" asked Kayin.

He was looking all around. Earnie was standing behind him, practically biting his pencil in half from fear.

"What? Where?" asked Earnie. "What was what? What was what?"

Earnie, Kayin and Officer McHale followed Kid Caramel's finger with their eyes. It pointed to the top of a great stone tower. "In that window over there by the tower...somebody's watching us!" yelled Caramel.

A small doorway at the base of the tower led to a spiral staircase. Caramel remembered, from his castle research, that the narrow stairway went up in a clockwise fashion. The design was to prevent invading swordsmen from swinging their blades as they made their way up. This made it easier to defend the tower. After all, how could a swordsman hit anything if he couldn't swing his sword, thought the boy detective.

"There is only one way to get to that window in the Great Hall. We have to go through half the castle to get there," said Kayin.

"Come on. Let's see if we can catch it!" Kid Caramel was already on his way inside the tower and up the spiraling stone stairs. He

41

slowed down to allow Kayin, who knew the castle's layout, to take the lead. Earnie followed closely behind but somehow managed to have his reporter's notepad out. If a ghost was going to take him out, he'd make sure he'd write about it for the paper.

McHale was just reaching the stone staircase, trying to catch up. He was waving his arms in the air frantically. "Boys, wait for me! I have to watch over you, remember?" Suddenly Officer McHale tripped on a stone step. He grabbed his ankle and leaned against the wall.

"I'll stay here and make sure nobody comes in," said Officer McHale, who was whining from the pain shooting out of his ankle. He was already on his walkie-talkie, calling for backup.

"OK! We'll be careful!" Kid Caramel yelled as he and his friends continued up the ancient stairs.

By the time the boys reached the top of the lower battlements, they were out of breath. The next set of stairs led into a huge arched wooden doorway. The doorway loomed at them like a dragon's wide-open mouth. It led across a curtain wall that had gaps every few feet called crenels. These were built so archers could hide behind the solid parts of the battlements, called merlons, as they took aim at targets below.

"This way," said Kayin. The boys entered the second tower and took the stairs down. A very narrow passage, built on a sharp right angle to slow down invaders, led toward a massive room. "This passage leads to the Great Hall and to the window. Maybe whatever or whoever it was left a clue behind."

The long and narrow passage was designed so that only one man could make his way into the tower at a time. This made it very difficult for an army to attack the castle during medieval times. The defenders of the castle had an easy time picking off invaders with arrows or with boiling water from the tiny holes called machicolations. Must have been one big ball of fun living back then, Caramel joked to himself. It seemed that every part of the castle was designed to put a hurtin' on people.

Inside the Great Hall, ten wooden torches in iron sconces hung from the walls. Suits of armor stood one to each of the ten thick stone columns supporting the walls. There was an elaborately embroidered carpet with different colored shields that ran along the fifty-foot length of the hall. Centuries ago, there would have been no carpet on the floor. Instead it would have been covered with grass and lavender. If an enemy archer shot a flaming arrow inside the castle, a fire would erupt if the hay was struck.

Kid Caramel noticed that he and his friends left deep footprints in the thick but worn carpet. He looked down at the carpet by the window.

"Guys, there aren't any footprints where the person we saw in the window was standing…that's definitely not a good thing!"

Suddenly, the massive oak double doors, the only way in or out of the Great Hall tower, slammed shut!

Chapter Five:
The Dungeon

"We're all gonna die!" yelled Kayin, who was pulling on the heavy metal door handle. Earnie pulled on the other handle to the double door but he had no luck either.

"No, we're not!" shouted Kid Caramel. "We've got to stay focused and find a way out of here, that's all." His sharp eyes looked over every nook and cranny of the gigantic room. There were eight beautiful stained glass windows, each depicting scenes of knights battling dragons above them. In the middle of the ceiling, which had to be 30 feet up, was a colossal candle chandelier. The chandelier was held in place by chains thicker than a python's body. None of these decorations were going to get them out of this room, thought the boy detective.

Kid Caramel started pressing his fingers along the gray stones in the wall. Each stone was over three feet thick to prevent anyone from entering the castle by battering the walls in. The invention of the cannon ended that hope and eventually led to the downfall of castle building.

"Maybe there's a secret switch hidden here somewhere," Caramel wondered aloud.

Earnie and Kayin pressed their fingers along the walls, too. Soon, everybody was turning over anything that wasn't nailed down. Pewter bowls that once held exotic fruits, ancient goblets that once contained expensive wine, and even the elaborately upholstered chairs, were ransacked. Kid Caramel even checked under the large oblong banquet table, made of pine and oak. The table, which could seat twelve, was where the lord and his advisors held important meetings. The castle had withstood countless invasions, but it had never been invaded by three scared boys.

Kayin sniffed at something in the air.

"Hey...guys...do you smell that?"

Kid Caramel sniffed the air while his hands kept feeling the nooks and crannies in the wall.

"Hmmm, yeah...I do smell something... could it be what I think it is?"

"I smell it too," added Earnie. "That smell reminds me of something...."

"Let's try to follow where it's coming from," said Kid Caramel. There were four huge hanging tapestries that covered a chunk of the far wall of the room. Each of the tapestries was embroidered with the McIntyre coat of arms, the large "M," two swords, a shield, and a wolf wearing a crown. Centered under one of the tapestries was a suit of armor holding a long jousting lance. It was the kind knights carried on horseback during competitions. The winner was the knight who knocked the opposing knight off the competitor's charging steed. On the wall next to the armor hung a shield and a pair of swords that were criss-crossed over each other.

Kid Caramel studied the fabric of each tapestry and then looked down at the carpet. The carpet was covered with dust and ingrained with ages of dirt. The impressions of hundreds of shoeprints, bootprints, and even animal prints were pushed into the fabric. All of the tapestries were dirty. But the third tapestry from the left had dozens of hand prints sunken into the plush fabric.

"Stand back, guys," said Kid Caramel as he tried to pull a sword from the wall display. The sword was probably just for show, but it was still quite heavy. From Caramel's research, wealthy young boys, or those born into nobility who wanted to be knights, had to practice wielding weapons until they were strong enough to carry them with confidence. These youths were called pages, and they served the lord of the castle while taking lessons in fighting and manners.

At age fourteen, they became squires and were the assistants to full knights. Squires helped the knights get into their elaborate, heavy armor before battles. If the squire proved himself worthy in battle, he would have the opportunity to become knighted by the king or another knight. If he was chosen, the king would have the squire kneel before him as he tapped him on the shoulder with his sword. When the young man rose, he was a knight, ready to serve his king.

Kid Caramel was not strong enough to lift the sword, so he tugged at the tapestry until it fell from its mooring.

"Wow, a secret passageway!" yelled

Kayin. He jumped in the air and kicked for joy. "I've been in this castle a zillion times and never even knew about it!"

"How'd you know, Kid?" asked Earnie, who never seemed to get used to Caramel's knack for finding what didn't want to be found.

"This tapestry, unlike the others, had all of these hand prints along the bottom and lower sides of it," Kid Caramel said, pointing to the hand prints. "Which meant someone was constantly moving it up or to the side to get to this passageway."

"And that smell is really coming strong from wherever this leads to," said Kayin.

Kid Caramel pulled a flashlight from his backpack and headed in. The others, now armed with flashlights as well, followed. The passageway was even more narrow than the stairwell, but this one had cables and wires leading into makeshift electrical outlets bolted to the stone walls. There was a warm orange flicker of lights at the other end and the smell became more powerful.

Slimy moss started to appear along the walls as the three boys exited the passageway.

They entered a dark room that groaned from ages of holding up the upper parts of the castle. The groans sounded like the voices of the dead. Every now and again drips of water echoed within the deepest parts of the castle.

"Now I think I know where we are," said Kayin with a gulp. He slowly moved his flashlight around the chamber. It was so cold they could see their breath. The dank smell of stagnant water stung their nostrils and the groans continued.

There were rusting chains hanging from the walls and ceiling, some with skeletons still dangling from their cold grip. Rats raced out of view as Kayin swung around the flashlight to reveal the rest of the chamber. One of the rats pushed a rotting yellow skull out of its path. Kid Caramel and Earnie felt their hearts skip a beat.

"You've got to be kidding me...this is the real dungeon!" said Kayin.

"What do you mean by the real dungeon, Kayin?" Earnie asked. A massive spider slinked into view behind Earnie. The spider looked like a hairy, beyond-nasty baseball and stalked back into the darkness behind Earnie's head. Kayin had to fight to keep from screaming like a maniac.

"We have a dungeon that tourists come to see, but it doesn't look like this at all. It's got fake cobwebs, a plastic iron maiden, and a rack. I read about the real dungeon but thought it had been sealed up a hundred years ago."

"Wow, so this is where the people who attacked the castle wound up," said Kid Caramel. "Cool!" he added.

The sound of someone coughing on the other side of a thick wooden door startled the group. Kayin aimed the light toward the door as the boys tiptoed across the room. Another, louder cough almost made them all jump out of their skins. The fat spider Kayin had seen earlier dropped to the floor in front of them and skitterred into a corner. It was the size of a cat, Kayin thought. This time the boys did yell at the top of their lungs and ran into the opposite corner of the room. Earnie's shoulder crashed into the wall. The sound of sliding stone filled the room as the wall spun around. The boys now found themselves in yet another secret passage at the top of an even darker stairwell. It looked like the entrance to a bottomless pit.

"Greeeat work with the shoulder, Earn',"

said Kid Caramel in a sarcastic tone.

"Thanks. I knew this passage was here all along," Earnie said. He grinned at the 'sure you did' faces Kayin and Caramel gave him. All three aimed their lights down the steps but there was still no end to the darkness below.

They walked slowly down the dark passageway. Kid Caramel could feel what seemed like millions of little crawling legs all over his body.

Along the passageway were even more thick cables and electrical outlets.

This time the smell from earlier was overwhelming. Whatever was at the bottom of these stairs was definitely the source of it. Finally the beam from Caramel's flashlight found another thick door, this time made of metal. Kayin's trembling hand reached for the thick handle and pulled the door open.

The light of a hundred lamps filled the dungeon as the door swung open all the way. Cables, wires, TV cameras, microphones, and catwalks were everywhere. It looked as if they had just walked onto a Hollywood movie set. At the other end of the room was another door.

This one was blocked by a large storage trunk.

The boys made their way to the trunk and lifted the lid.

Earnie counted off the inventory. "It's full of make-up, fake fangs, paint, and about a hundred glass jars." Earnie held up one of the jars. It was filled with a green goo.

"We saw that same stuff, what did you call it...ectoplasm on the windshield of my dad's car," said Kayin.

"Yup, it matches," said Earnie as he compared the contents of the jar with the stuff he'd scooped up into the sandwich bag at the airport.

"This is some kind of movie set...but what in the world is it doing in the castle dungeon?" Caramel asked. He popped a piece of bubblegum into his mouth and paced the room. He was now in "Supercomputer Brainiac Mode." Under the lights and cameras was a very long pine table. There were plates piled sky-high filled with gobs of food. A gigantic turkey smothered in stuffing and gravy sauce hogged the table. Platters of yams, rice, vegetables, and nuts completed the spread.

"I knew I smelled something familiar...a home-cooked dinner," said Earnie, his tongue hanging out of his mouth like a hungry dog.

All the way at the end, seated at the head of the table, was a figure shrouded in shadow. It made sounds like he was stuffing the food down his throat like there was no tomorrow. It would choke every so often, releasing a cackling cough.

Slowly, Kayin took steps toward it. Both Caramel and Earnie were at his side as he got closer and closer. Then the figure stopped and pointed at them!

"Hahahahah! At last!" it said as it continued to point. All at once, the boys aimed their flashlights at the mysterious figure.

The lights revealed an elderly man, with white hair and a red bushy beard. Chunks of food were stuck in his beard. He flashed the boys a crooked smile filled with meat and vegetables. Earnie took cover behind Kid Caramel.

"Grandpa...is it really you?" Kayin asked over the barrage of noise that was the old man's eating and drinking. The old man stopped mid-swallow. He put a hand over his eyebrows to block the flashlights.

"I would be the very legend himself, Kayin, m'lad!"

Kayin ran into his arms, knocking over a tray of roasted chestnuts and two bottles of wine. Even seated Grandpa McIntyre looked to be as tall as Kayin's father.

"We came to rescue you from the evil ghosts, Grandpa," said Kayin. He wiped a tear from his eye and toughened himself up. After all, the other guys were watching.

"Evil whatsis? What in the murky lochs are you jabbering on about, boy?"

"When you didn't come home, father called the police. They came to the castle to get you and only found your talisman. So, we came to rescue you," Kayin explained. He watched in shock as his grandfather reached around his neck. His grandfather was still wearing his talisman.

"No, m'boy, I'm afraid I haven't been kidnapped. I was told that I was going to be the star of a new commercial to advertise the castle attractions," said Kayin's grandfather. He pointed to a picture on the wall. "These fancy-smancy movie producers hired me."

Kid Caramel leaned next to the picture.

There was a woman in an expensive-looking outfit standing next to a director's chair. The man had a mustache and a baseball cap turned backward. Behind them stood the film crew.

"Wait a minute...I recognize those people...." Caramel put his fingers over the mustache in the photo.

"What are you saying, junior?" asked Grandpa McIntyre.

A voice came from the passageway. "What he'ssss ssssaying issss that all of you know too mucccchhh about my plansssss."

In stepped the dark ghost who had taunted the boys earlier. It was holding the jousting lance from the suit of armor and pointing it straight at Kid Caramel.

"What would you be planning on doing with that wee stick, sonny?" asked Grandpa McIntyre angrily. He rolled up his sleeves and loosened the top buttons on his shirt.

"I'm going to make a human sssshish-kabob out offf all of you. That way I'll be ssssure to get you all out of my hair...permanently."

Earnie leaped under the table in world-record time. Grandpa McIntyre gently pushed Kayin and Caramel behind his back to protect them.

56

The dark ghost ran toward the boys, leveling the lance at them. The boys scattered in different directions as the phantom chased them. Food went flying every which way, splattering the dungeon walls. Some of it landed on the skeletons, knocking bones loose. Long dead fingers, skulls, and kneecaps crashed to the floor, raising clouds of ancient dust. Rats scurried, trying to find a safe place to hide amid the chaos.

Grandpa McIntyre jumped up on the pine table. He kicked the plates of food out of his way as he ran toward the fake ghost. The old man jumped in the air from the table and launched himself at the ghost. The two fell onto the floor in a cloud of fists, bones, dust, rats, and splinters of lance wood. When the dust settled, Grandpa McIntyre was seated on top of the ghost, who was struggling to get free.

Kid Caramel walked up to the ghost and yanked at the hood covering its head.

"No way!" said Kid Caramel. "He's no ghost...that's Mr. Cragmire! He's the guy on the poster with your grandpa!" he continued. "And the lady is your wife! Look at the photo on the wall, guys, both he and Mrs. Cragmire are wearing the same wedding bands!"

"Well, well, freakin' well. You kids got lucky this time, that's all," said Mr. Cragmire as Grandpa tied him up with some of the cables on the floor.

"Grandpa, are you OK?" asked Kayin.

"Boy, I may be older than the Highlands, but I ain't dead. I used to scrap with the best of 'em when I was your age, lad. And I still got it!"

Kayin's face turned red when he remembered an important detail. "Oh, my gosh! We have to get to Mrs. Cragmire's office. Father is signing the castle away to be sold to a crook!"

"What? Well, let's go, lads. I can still drive like a banshee on fire!" said Grandpa McIntyre. He rounded up the crew and they raced through the castle. No sooner than exiting the ancient structure did they pile into Grandpa's car, buckled up, and hit the road.

Chapter Six:
Mach 5 Grandpa

When Grandpa McIntyre jammed his foot on the gas pedal, Caramel thought he was back on the airplane again. He and the other boys were pushed into their chairs by the sheer pressure of the station wagon (which had to be at least as old as Grandpa was) going from zero to Mach 5 in one second flat. Compared to the way Grandpa drove, warp speed seemed like a leisurely jog through the park on a Sunday afternoon, thought Caramel.

They zipped through the trees, well off the highway, on a path that Grandpa seemed to make up as he went along. They crushed plants, grass, small logs, and Caramel thought maybe a sheep or two. The speeding car plowed through a prize-winning flower garden, whipped past hazel and rowan trees, through the shallow

...rt of a loch, up a very bumpy mountain (just missing a herd of red deer), and across a broken stone bridge.

Caramel and Kayin were hootin' and hollerin' and giving each other high-fives with each stunt. Earnie had turned into a statue again and was on the verge of passing out.

Meanwhile, across town...

Mr. McIntyre parked the minivan on High Street, several stores down from Eastgate Shopping Center. He and Mr. Parks entered the Law Offices of Cragmire & Cragmire. There wasn't a receptionist to greet them, which both men found strange.

Mr. McIntyre knocked lightly on the reception desk. "Hello? Is anyone in?"

A few moments later, they heard footsteps approaching. It was a woman in her late forties. She looked both men over for a second or two then took out a pack of cigarettes.

"Mr. McIntyre, how nice to see you again." She then turned to Mr. Parks and offered her hand. "I'm Nairne Cragmire. Sorry to have kept you gentlemen waiting."

"Ronald Parks," said Mr. Parks, introducing himself.

"Please follow me to my office so I can see what I can do for you."

Mrs. Cragmire offered the men seats and soft drinks or coffee. She then took her own plush seat at her desk.

"I need to sell off the McIntyre Castle due to a family emergency," said Mr. McIntyre.

"Does this have anything to do with your father?" she asked. "It's all over the news."

"Yes, but please, we have less than fifteen minutes to post the castle for sale on the Internet."

Mrs. Cragmire smoked long thin cigarettes and the smoke burned Mr. Parks's eyes. She nodded and opened the file cabinet next to the window. After searching through several folders, she took out a set of documents. She slid the documents and a pen over to Mr. McIntyre.

Mr. McIntyre handed the papers to Mr. Parks. "My friend here is also an attorney and I just want him to take a look before I sign," said Mr. McIntyre.

Mrs. Cragmire looked annoyed at the news but kept her calm. She stood, walked behind Mr. Parks, and puffed away on her cigarette.

"On our drive here, Wallace told me that you and Mr. Cragmire were handling the bills for the castle tourism business," said Mr. Parks.   "I'd like to see those, please."

Caramel's father read over the contract to sell the castle. The contract was well written and looked legal. Having Mrs. Cragmire standing less than one foot away from him didn't make reading the contract any easier. She kept tapping her toe on the floor as if she was very nervous about something.

"I'd like to see the unpaid bills, please," said Mr. Parks again.

She finally handed them over to him and tapped her toe even faster.

"Is there something wrong?" asked Mrs. Cragmire, blowing that toxic smoke into his face. Mr. Parks coughed and fanned the bitter smoke clouds away with the contract.

"What I don't understand is why the bills came directly to you and they went unpaid. The financial records prove that the tourism from the castle made more than enough money to pay all of the bills twice over."

"What?" asked Mr. McIntyre in shock. "Is this true, Nairne?"

"I know what I'm doing, Mr. McIntyre. There are many other factors that go into paying for a tourism business. Legal fees, for example."

"So, instead of paying the bills, your law firm took your share first, which left no money for the rest of the bills. Is that correct?" Mr. Parks asked.

"Is there a problem with that?" said Mrs. Cragmire angrily. "I have to eat too." She walked to her desk and slid open a drawer.

"I see now!" yelled Kayin's father. "It's because of you bloody leeches that my business is going down the drain! You want me to sell the castle so you can keep all the money from the tourism and pay yourself tons of my money!"

"Not so fast, gentlemen," said Mrs. Cragmire, who pulled something out of the desk. She pointed a stun gun at them. "I'm taking that castle and neither of you are going to stop me. Now sign the papers!" She put the stun gun close to Mr. McIntyre's face.

Mr. McIntyre and Mr. Parks exchanged worried glances and then looked at the stun gun. There really didn't seem to be any other choice. Mr. McIntyre slowly brought the pen to the contract and began to sign it.

Suddenly, a station wagon plowed into the office and the front door shattered into a million pieces.

Everyone ran for cover. The car hadn't even come to a complete stop when Grandpa McIntyre rolled out of the driver's seat and into the room. He tossed what was left of the jousting lance at the stun gun, pinning it to the wall.

"What is it with you Cragmires? You got midges eating your brains?" asked Grandpa McIntyre. He rolled up his sleeves in case he had to get into another scrap.

Mr. Parks handed the contract to Wallace McIntyre. Mr. McIntyre ripped it to shreds and threw the pieces of paper in the air.

"Oh, Ronald, this is my father, Ewan McIntyre," said Kayin's father. "He's a retired commander from our special police, Scotland Yard."

"Nice to meet you, son. Now let me and this detective lad, Caramel, fill you fellas in on this whole shenanigan...."

*　　*　　*　　*

"So, you were aware of the Cragmires' scheme to buy the castle the whole time, Grandpa?" asked Kayin.

"Bet yer bagpipes I was. Older does not mean slower or dumber, laddie. I'm still sharper than a tack on a good day. I was wondering what took you so long to come and get me. I was getting fat from all the food they were giving me down in that dungeon."

"So, the longer they kept you in the dungeon, the more desperate the family would get to sell the castle," said Kid Caramel.

"You got it, kid," answered Grandpa. "The Cragmires were gonna use all of this film equipment to create ghosts with fancy-smancy special effects," said Grandpa.

"Wow, and all of those ghosts would increase the tourism once they owned the castle," said Kid Caramel.

"Yer sharp as a sword, kid," said Grandpa.

65

"Everybody wants to see ghosts. Now give me a second while I put some shiny handcuffs on my friend, Mrs. Cragmire. You are under arrest, Miss."

Kayin and his dad hugged Grandpa and he shooshed them away. He was old, but didn't go for all that mushy stuff. Now Kayin knew where he got that from and laughed.

* * * *

"How'd you know that I was a detective, Mr. McIntyre?" asked Kid Caramel as he carefully returned his badge to the backpack. They were all heading back to the castle in the warp-enabled station wagon. Grandpa McIntyre had to meet the investigators from Scotland Yard at the castle to turn the Cragmires in. Mrs. Cragmire had passed out from Grandpa's crazy driving.

"Kayin never stops yapping and e-mailing us all about you and Earnie," said Grandpa. "And about some Sharktooth fella. I'd like to show that little punk a thing or two myself."

They all laughed as Grandpa stepped on the brake in front of the castle. They stopped so abruptly that the seatbelts almost snapped.

They piled out of the station wagon at the foot of the dirt path which led to the draw-bridge. It was nighttime now and the moon was almost full. The castle cast a long and eerie shadow almost to the shore of the loch. As the party made their way up the path to the main entrance, Caramel stumbled and fell.

His eyes opened wider than the moon when he looked at what he had tripped over.

"Uh, guys...you won't believe what I just found."

Under Caramel's leg was the print of a large, finned animal. The shape was like the fin of a seal or a sea lion, but much, much larger. The creature must have been heavy because the print was pressed down five inches into the mud. As he looked around, he noticed dozens more, all leading out of the loch and into the woods.

"That print's gotta be at least three feet long!" yelled Earnie. He had already pulled out a tape measure and his notepad. Kayin took out a small notepad and began to sketch the print.

"Could it be...something like Nessie over in Loch Ness?" asked Kayin with a grin on his freckled face.

67

"Uh, Dad...I think we're gonna have to stay in Scotland for one more week," said Caramel. He pinned his badge back onto his jacket, then stuck a piece of banana bubblegum in his mouth and passed the pack around. This time even his father and Mr. McIntyre and Grandpa took a piece.

Afterword by the author

Hey, mystery fans, this is Dwayne (but my friends call me Hunter). I visited Scotland in 1985 and actually went to Loch Ness to look for Nessie. Let me tell you that Loch Ness is every bit as creepy as it looks in the photos.

I would highly recommend that you read some books on cool myths like Nessie, Sasquatch, UFOs, and other unexplained stuff. The more you read, the smarter you become. And being smart is beyond cool!

Well, I'm hard at work on the next books in the **KID CARAMEL**™ series. I want to thank all of you for joining us in this mystery. We all look forward to having another cool adventure with you soon. See ya!

Hunter

P.S. Drop me a line and let me know what you think of the **KID CARAMEL**™ series. You can send fan art and letters to me at Just Us Books and I'll put them up on the **KID CARAMEL**™ section of my web site!!!

www.justusbooks.com
www.diehardstudio.com

Dwayne J. Ferguson is a writer and artist, creator of the Captain Africa series, and illustrator of *AFRO-BETS*® *Coloring and Activity Book*. He loves computer games and when he's not developing characters of his own, he enjoys teaching students how to create computer graphics. Dwayne operates his own design studio and makes his home with his wife in northern New Jersey.

Tell Us What You Think About **KID CARAMEL**™

Name _____

Address _____

City _____ State _____ Zip_____

Birthdate_____ Grade_____

Teacher's Name _____

School _____

Write down the title of this book. _____

_____

Who is your favorite character in this book? Do you
know of anyone like Kid Caramel? Or Earnie? _____

_____

_____

What mysteries or cases would you like to see treated
in future KID CARAMEL™ books? _____

_____

_____

How did you get your first copy of
KID CARAMEL?™
Parent? Gift? Teacher? Library? Friend? Other?

_____

Are you looking forward to the next title in this series?
Why, or why not? _____

_____

Any other comments? _____

_____

Send your reply to:
KID CARAMEL™ c/o Just Us Books, Inc.
356 Glenwood Avenue, East Orange, NJ 07017

**More Great Books for Middle Readers
Look for these other Just Us Books titles:**

Kid Caramel: Private Investigator
Book #1 Case of the Missing Ankh
Book #2 The Werewolf of PS 40
Book #3 Mess at Loch Ness
Book #4 Ghost Ranch: The Legend of Mad Jake
by Dwayne J. Ferguson

NEATE To the Rescue by Debbi Chocolate
NEATE: Elizabeth's Wish by Debbi Chocolate
NEATE: Anthony's Big Surprise by Wade Hudson
NEATE: Eddie's Ordeal by Kelly Starling Lyons
NEATE: A Test for Tayesha by Tara Demps Soyinka

Dear Corinne, Tell Somebody! Love Annie
by Mari Evans

A Blessing in Disguise
by Eleanora E. Tate
Just An Overnight Guest
by Eleanora E. Tate

visit us at www.justusbooks.com